TRUST

Jana Aston

Edited by RJ Locksley
Cover Design by JA Huss
Formatting by Erik Gevers

I **DONUT** know what id do
without a reader like you!

Dedication

To Chelcie, for trusting herself.

One

Chloe

"Look at us. We are so ladies who lunch." Everly glances at the waitress. "Can I have tea, love? Do you have tea with a proper cup and saucer?" Everly blinks at the waitress in complete sincerity while the poor woman smiles politely and replies that they just have regular mugs. The four of us—Sophie, Sandra, Everly and myself—have met for lunch at the Italian restaurant located in the building Sophie lives in. We just sat down, so I'm not sure yet why Everly is speaking in the worst attempt at a British accent I've ever heard.

"She'll have an iced tea—in a regular glass. Thank you." I cut Everly off and smile at the waitress, who happily accepts my interference and bolts. It's warm inside the restaurant so I slip out of the sweater I put on before I left the house. You never can predict how the weather will behave in October, so it's best to be prepared.

"Cheerio, Chloe, thank you for ordering for me."

"Why in the hell are you suddenly British?" I lower my menu and stare at her.

"She's practicing," Sandra says. "Sawyer's taking her to London with him on a business trip."

"I can't imagine anyone really speaks like that in

London," I say drily.

"They might, mates, they might." Everly looks hopefully around the table while Sandra, Sophie and I stare at her, unconvinced. "Am I getting any better, loves?"

"You might want to work on that a bit longer," Sophie suggests. "Or maybe just get a hat. They wear a lot of hats in the UK, don't they?"

"Oh, holy shit, I am getting a fascinator!" Everly drops the accent and her face lights up as she waves her hands around in excitement.

"Here we go," I mumble. "Thanks, Sophie."

"Do you think I can get one online? Or do you think I should wait till I get there to buy one?" Everly's eyes widen. "Do you think I can pull off a feather?"

"You should definitely wait," Sophie tells her, setting down her menu. "Definitely not to the feather. Now pick something to eat. I'm starving. And if you try to order fish and chips in an Italian restaurant I will punch you in the face."

"Tsk, tsk, someone's a little crabby," Everly complains.

"I'm not crabby, I'm pregnant. So freaking pregnant. I've been pregnant for a year. I know it's nine months, blah blah, but guess how long nine months is in gestation time? I'll tell you, it's an eon. My ankles are swollen, my boobs are ginormous, my back aches and I'm big enough to be carrying a litter, but no, my doctor and my husband both insist there's only one baby in there." She finishes her rant pointing to her stomach. "One!"

We all stop looking at our menus to look at Sophie. She's adorable, actually. She looks good pregnant, even if she doesn't think so. Her stomach is indeed huge—she's due in less than two weeks—but it looks like she's got a basketball shoved under her shirt. She's all limbs and bump.

"Yeah, about that." Everly waves at Sophie's stomach. "How is the sex with that thing?" The question is directed at Sophie, but Sandra blushes and I groan.

Sophie doesn't even blink. Apparently growing a human reduces your embarrassment threshold. "I'm horny all the time," Sophie wails in a whisper. "All the freaking time. Luke says it's the hormones and perfectly normal, but I don't think it's normal. I think I'm a pregnant pervert."

"So like…" Everly looks at her seriously, smoothing her long dark hair over her shoulders and leaning in closer. "Doggie style?"

Sandra and I glance at each other, then to Sophie. Fine, I'm curious. That bump is huge.

"For a while, but my boobs got so big it hurts when they bounce. So now I cowgirl him and make him hold my boobs with his hands."

Huh. Well, then.

"Well, I am never having children," Everly proclaims, eyeing Sophie's bump warily, "but I might cowgirl Sawyer when I get home."

"You have a child," I remind her.

"Obviously, Chloe," she replies, waving her hand at me dismissively. "And Jake is the most perfect kid anyone could ever hope for. But he arrived already walking, talking and potty-trained." She looks at Sophie's giant bump again with genuine concern in her eyes. "I wonder if Sawyer has any other secret baby mommas." She says this hopefully, like only she could. "A little girl would be super fun if I didn't have to push her out of my vagina."

Sophie's the first one of us to have a baby, even though Everly has a five-year-old son, Jake. Everything is happening so fast. Well, for my friends anyway. Sophie met Luke last fall during our senior year at Penn. She was pregnant and married before graduation. Everly met Sawyer last Thanksgiving and they were married over the summer. Sawyer's son from a previous relationship lives with them full-time and Everly adapted to insta-motherhood better than anyone could have expected. She's working on a children's book series about blended families now. Weird, I know. I always assumed she'd write porn. And then there's Sandra; she's a few years older than us. Sandra works for Everly's husband and quickly became a part of our friendship circle, or squad, as Everly prefers we call it. Sandra started dating Gabe at the beginning of the year and was living with him by summer.

That leaves me.

Chloe Scott. Third wheel, or seventh wheel in this case.

It's not that I haven't tried. I have. It's just that I'm super awkward. Plus dating is hard.

I've been stood up. I've been sent dick pics—more unsolicited dick pics than I can count. I mean, what is with that? How does that seem like a good idea? I deleted the first one figuring it was a random loony. After the third one I checked my online dating profile, wondering if I'd somehow checked a box requesting penis pictures. I couldn't even find an option for that.

Once a guy forgot my name—in the middle of our date. Just last month I went out with a guy who asked me if I wanted to have sex before dinner. I'm not even kidding. I met him at seven outside of the restaurant and he mentioned our dinner reservation was at nine. I was confused, but I put a smile on my face, thinking he'd actually forgotten to get a reservation and now we had to wait till nine. No biggie. But no. He told me he lived around the corner from there and he thought we could go back to his place before dinner. Because, and I quote, "It's not good to have sex on a full stomach."

I'd met him online a few weeks earlier—having joined a dating website in my quest to fulfil my being-an-adult checklist:

Graduate with honors.
Secure a full-time teaching position.
Find an apartment.
Learn how to date.

I'd felt comfortable with him. I'd enjoyed talking to him both online and eventually over the phone, and he was one of the few who hadn't sent an unsolicited dick pic. So when he'd asked me if he could take me to dinner I'd readily agreed.

Then he made the comment about having sex on a full stomach. I was about to make a sarcastic joke, thinking he was kidding, when he continued. "They have great steak here, but I can't eat red meat before sex, so I thought we could do sex before dinner instead of after."

Totally. Serious.

I about had a heart attack because in my limited experience I don't know what one says to that. Besides no thank you, obviously. But I hate rejecting people. I hate it. I teach the second grade. I'm all about kindness and inclusion and not hurting feelings. Which is stupid, I know. Bad behavior does not deserve a reward. That's what I tell my classroom. *Be kind, class. Treat each of your classmates as a friend. Compliment each other. If you know something, share. If you can help someone, help.* When they do, they earn classroom coins that they can exchange for special prizes in my classroom store. When they're unkind to a classmate they lose a coin.

But those rules don't apply to dating. So while I wanted to ask my date to hand over his coins, I'm not sure it would have been effective—or given the message intended. But I wasn't putting out to spare someone's feelings. So I made it clear I wasn't having sex with him on the first date. I tried that once, in college. No lie, the guy didn't remember having sex with me the next day—or pretended he didn't. Neither of which was great for my self-esteem.

So I'd declined his offer to have sex before dinner and he'd declined taking me to dinner. He'd left, and I'd gone home and eaten ramen noodles. Which is fine, it's not that tragic. Ramen noodles are delicious.

I was on a dating site once before. Everly, my college roommate, signed me up without my knowledge. Apparently I had a lot of interest based on a profile I didn't fill out and conversations I wasn't having. My bestie, posing as me, was very popular. Later, she would try to tell me that it was practically the same as me being popular, but I wasn't buying it. She did get me to go on a date disguised as a tutoring session. How she got the guy to meet me in a college library I'll never know. It took me twenty minutes to realize he didn't need tutoring in sophomore English, that he had in fact graduated with a degree in engineering four years prior. It took another five minutes for me to explain to him that I wasn't the girl he'd been chatting with online and apologize for my roommate's well-meaning interference.

I wasn't interested in Everly's matchmaking. College was for studying, preparing for the future. Plus Everly thinks with her heart, not her head, and where did that ever get anyone? I mean, yes, she did marry a billionaire who's crazy in love with her... okay, never mind, my point sucks. But I'm not Everly. Flying by the seat of your pants and thinking with your heart works for girls like Everly, but not for girls like me. Men gravitate towards Everly. I send off warning signals that say, *Too much work.* Anyway, I don't need a man or anything. I might want one, but I don't *need* one. I'm capable of taking care of myself. I don't need anyone to save me or fix my life. Totally ridiculous. I don't need flowers and butterflies, I really don't.

I graduated in May, moved into my own apartment in June and started my job as a second-grade teacher in August. I'm totally nailing life.

Except...

Except dating isn't any easier than it was in high school. Or college. Meaning it's not great. Dating is basically three hours of talking to a stranger, which is stupid, right? I don't enjoy that. I mean who enjoys that? Who? Who are those people? It's weird. Dating is weird.

And as much as I don't *need* a man, it'd be *nice* to have one. I'll get better at dating though, I will. Practice makes perfect, right? That's what I tell my students. They learn something new every week and it's not always easy. Some lessons are trickier than others. Some kids learn at a different pace than others, and that's okay. So I'm not as good at dating as my friends are. I'll figure it out. Eventually.

The waitress stops back and takes our orders and the second she leaves Everly turns her attention on me.

"So, how's the dating going?" Everly asks. "Have you gotten any more POD's?"

"What's a POD?" I ask her, confused.

"Proof of dick," Everly says with a nod when we all stare at her.

7

"Is that what it's called now?" Sophie asks while rubbing the side of her bump with a grimace.

"Not yet," Everly says while swirling the straw in her glass. "But I'm trying to make it catch on. It's a little classier than 'dick pic', don't you think?" She takes a sip of her iced tea and then sets the glass down, brows raised as we all stare at her. "What?"

"How exactly are you intending to make it catch on?"

"I'm so glad you asked, Chloe. The thing is, I'm married, so no one is sending me POD's anymore," she begins.

"Right," I agree. "I would hope not."

"But you, my friend, are still dating, so I thought you could—"

"No," I interrupt. "No. Stop talking."

"All you need to do," she continues anyway, "is reply to the dick pics you get and say, 'Nice POD.' Or even, 'Nice POD, LOL.'"

"Nope, not doing it. I am not going to encourage dick pics so you can coin a new phrase. No."

"Okay, no problem," she says with a shrug. She's quiet for exactly three seconds before her mouth opens again. "How about, 'Why are you sending me a POD?' That way you're still delivering the branding message, but without the encouragement."

I stuff a forkful of pasta into my mouth, glare at Everly and shake my head no.

"Well, I think it's catchy."

"Why do men do that?" I ask, glancing around the table in disbelief. "Do you know how many dick pics—"

"POD's!" Everly interrupts.

"POD's I get sent with nothing more than two words exchanged? They say 'hey,' I reply back 'hi,' and the next thing they send is a picture of their dick. It's bizarre."

"They want to prove they have a dick, obviously. In case you were worried they're a eunuch." Everly states this calmly, like it's a reasonable explanation, while the rest of us stare at her. "Funny story, I was actually worried Sawyer might be a eunuch because he made me wait like, all night to have sex on our first date."

That story is greeted by the three of us staring at her, silent.

"What? He's not. I mean, he's really not, if you know what I mean. He's the opposite of—"

"We get it, Everly. Thank you."

"Anyway," Everly continues with her story. "A lot of men catfish their dick pics, so the only way to verify is in person anyway."

"What?" I ask, tilting my head at her in confusion.

"You know, when they send a picture of some random dick from the internet, because it's bigger than theirs."

"No." I shake my head. "Does that really happen?"

"All the time," Everly says, nodding confidently. "I saw an article on it. On a blog."

"Anyway," Sophie interjects and turns to me. "Back to Chloe. How is the dating going?" She reaches behind her and rubs at her back while she talks.

"Well, I got asked to fuck a guy with a strap-on," I mumble and stuff a piece of bread into my mouth.

"I'm sorry?" Everly asks, leaning forward. Sophie shifts in her chair uncomfortably, rubbing her bump, and Sandra sighs, because she's already heard this story. Everly's my best friend, but Sandra is my dating confidante. Everly is filled with good intentions, but she's... a little invasive. She's forever trying to set me up with guys she's picked out and it's just too much pressure. Plus if she actually managed to set me up with someone I liked she'd be so smug about it. And she'd probably follow me on the dates to watch and text me pointers.

So I talk to Sandra about these things. She's been on the receiving end of Everly's matchmaking shenanigans, so she gets it. Sandra is very discreet. I can send her all the details of the guy I'm meeting and know that she'll never use it, unless I actually do disappear while on a date. Everly on the other hand would use the information to Facebook-friend the guy, run a background check and befriend his mother. So Sandra is the one I send the details to. You know, the safety details—who I'm meeting, when, where etc. I watch a lot of crime television, specifically *Criminal Minds*, so I always make sure someone knows where I am if I'm meeting a date. Just in case he turns out to be a criminal or whatever.

"A strap-on," I repeat. "Penis," I clarify when no one speaks.

I'm met with silence. I glance around the table at their shocked faces and then stuff another bite of pasta in my mouth while shrugging again.

"I'm gonna need you to back this story up," Everly says while holding both hands up and bending her fingers towards her like she's directing traffic. "Back. It. Up."

"Yeah, I think we're going to need more information," Sophie agrees.

"I got a match on the dating app I'm using. The guy is gorgeous. He messages me immediately and I'm all hell yeah, fist-pumping myself in my living room. The message says, 'One question. Will you fuck me with a strap-on?'" I pause and look around the table. "So I think he's joking and type back, 'Only if I can pick the size,' and I'm proud of myself for being so quick on my feet, you know? I'm sitting on my couch laughing when his next message comes in. It said, 'Any size you want. I'll buy.' He was serious. That's what dating looks like. Men messaging and asking if I want to fuck them with a strap-on. I think it's me. I attract weirdos."

"I don't think it's you," Sophie says soothingly while Everly shakes her head in agreement.

"No, I think it's me."

"Once—back when I was single—a guy left in the middle of sex," Sandra says and we all swivel our attention to her.

"Stop!" Everly throws her hand up. "I know you're shy but I cannot believe you've kept this story from me when I've known you almost a year. A year!"

Sandra blushes and covers her eyes with her hand. "It's embarrassing."

"Too late. I need the details."

"So this guy, we went out a few times. I thought it was going well, you know?" She glances around the table. "We met for coffee a couple of times. Met for drinks at this really cute place another time and it turned into dinner. I thought we had something."

"And then…?" Everly asks, drawing the words out.

"We had sex. Halfway through he stopped, pulled out and left."

"That is not a true story," Everly says.

"It is." Sandra nods. "I promise you it is."

"Was he still hard?"

"Yup. Pulled out. Pulled up his pants and left. I never heard from him again."

The table is silent again while we mull that over. Then Sophie reminds us that she dated a gay guy for two years.

"Dating sucks," I conclude.

"I got kicked out a guy's apartment once," Everly offers as her contribution to dating horror stories.

"You broke into his apartment, Everly. You stole his key and broke in. You're *his* dating horror story, not the other way around," I remind her while Sophie and Sandra laugh.

"Minor detail, Chloe." Everly groans. "It was still a painful learning experience. Anyway, enough doom and gloom. I've got the perfect guy in mind for you."

"Of course you do. No."

"He's hot—and he's FBI. Everyone knows you have that Fed fetish. I bet he owns handcuffs," she adds, with a dramatic wink. "And there is no way he's bad in bed. No way. You know how you can just tell sometimes by looking at a guy? Just by the way he moves? That's what you need. A guy who knows what he's doing in bed. And at the very least this guy is packing."

"Wait. Are you talking about my brother?" Sophie interjects. Sophie has a half-brother I've never met.

"Obviously, Sophie. How many federal agents do I know?" Everly responds in a 'duh' tone of voice.

"It's actually a great idea, but please do not talk about my brother's junk in front of me. It's disgusting." Sophie winces and rubs at her baby bump. "I think Boyd's a bit of a player though. He's never even introduced me to anyone he's seeing. But good plan. You guys talk about it. I'm going to the restroom." She pushes back her chair and stands, then immediately sits again, looking at us in a panic. "I think my water just broke."

"I've got this," Everly announces, waving her hands excitedly as she flags down the waitress. "I'm gonna need a pot of boiling water, some towels and the check."

"Oh, my God," Sophie mutters and digs her cell phone out of her purse.

"Just the check," I tell the waitress. I turn back to Everly as Sophie calls her husband. "You're not delivering Sophie's baby, Everly. Her water broke ten seconds ago and her husband—the gynecologist—is in their condo upstairs. So even if this baby was coming in the next five minutes, which it is not, you're still not delivering it at a table in Serafina."

Everly slumps in her chair and shakes her head. "I've been watching YouTube videos on childbirth for months, just in case. What a waste." She sighs, then perks up. "Can I at least be in the delivery room?"

"No," we all respond in unison.

Sophie's husband Luke walks in a few minutes later. They live on the top floor of this high-rise so he was only an elevator ride away. He places his hand softly on the back of Sophie's neck and bends down, murmuring something into her ear. She blinks and nods as he kisses her temple before standing, holding up a long coat for her to slip into, discreetly hiding the fact that her water just broke.

"I cannot believe this just happened in a restaurant," Sophie mumbles as Luke wraps the coat around her.

Sandra, Everly and I sit back in our chairs and glance at each other, a little stunned at the whirlwind of the last few minutes, until finally Everly speaks.

"Well, that's official. I am never giving birth. Like ever."

Two

Chloe

I've never been good at dating. In high school I got a boyfriend by default—my best friend was dating his best friend and poof, there you go. I'm not sure Dave even asked me out, we were always just shoved together. I liked Dave and it was nice to have a date for school dances and whatnot. But I don't know if I learned anything about dating from that.

College wasn't much better. I dabbled enough to decide that my time was better spent studying, figuring there'd be time later for dating. I was at Penn on a scholarship and it was essential that I kept my grades up. So now here I am. I've got a college degree, an apartment and a job. And no idea how to date. In my defense, the dating pool thus far has been dismal. But I've got another date tonight and it needs to go well because I can't take another rejection or weird situation. A girl can only handle so many strap-on requests.

I'm sort of hopelessly bad at this. Last week I went out with a guy for drinks. It was the first time we'd met and I was nervous. Dating gives me anxiety. Most social situations give me anxiety, but dating is worse. What on earth would we talk about? But then I reminded myself that everyone likes to be complimented. It's something I work on with my class—if you notice something nice about someone, tell them. So I'd walked in and yelled, "I like your pants." Yeah. It's actually worse than it sounds. The week before that I went out with a guy whose name was Rick Martin and I... I blurted out, "*Living La Vida Loca*," and did a weird dance. So clearly there's room for improvement.

I survey myself in the mirror and will my racing heart to calm. I can do this. I can totally do this. *It's just a date, Chloe.* I remind myself that there's no need to be nervous. People go on dates every day—for fun. I don't think it's fun, but people do. My friends do. It's just that I tend to be awkward and come across as sarcastic when I don't mean to be.

So today needs to go well. I just... I really need it to. I'm going on a date to a Philadelphia Eagles game and I have high hopes. It's technically my second date with this guy since I met him last weekend for coffee. I like this guy, Cal. He's a fireman and he's really cute. A fireman and a school teacher—sounds like a perfect match, doesn't it? And it was good, the coffee date. I don't want to jinx it, but I think we could have something.

I check my reflection again, jeans and a long-sleeved knit shirt in a green that matches both my eyes and the team colors of the Eagles. The sleeves are long. They reach the middle of my hand and there's a hole in each cuff to slip over my thumb. I wonder if there's a term for that hole. It's weird, right? A hole sewn into the seam of a long-sleeved shirt to slip your thumb through thus keeping the sleeves pulled down low. Weird. I'll have to Google it later. But right now, Cal is picking me up. I grab my wristlet and head downstairs to the building lobby to wait for him.

***

"We got an interesting call at the firehouse yesterday," Cal tells me as we make the drive to the stadium. Luckily the traffic isn't bad on the Schuylkill and we're making good time. The stadium is less than six miles from my apartment, but you never know how traffic is going to be on game days.

"What happened?" I ask, turning my head in his direction. I'm interested in his story and it gives me the chance to watch him talk. He's cute, very boy-next-door. He's not very tall, but he's several inches taller than me. A little on the stocky side, with thick dark hair, a little messy. He's wearing shorts—like only a guy would in late September—and a Philadelphia Eagles jersey. His sunglasses block the midday sun but I can see the corner of his eye as he talks.

"A call came in—motor vehicle vs toddler."

"Oh, how awful."

He pulls his hand from the steering wheel and says, "Just wait," with a little shake of his head and a smile. "So we arrive on scene and there's no car. No one is even outside. Nothing, right? Usually there's a crowd, but it's just us. Then the ambulance and the cops pull up right behind us. We all get out and look at each other for a second before one of our guys goes up to the house as one of the cops is checking the street for tire marks. So a teenager answers the door and lets us inside. Turns out the motor vehicle was a matchbox car one kid threw at another and the mom called 911 for a flesh wound."

"No!" I say, laughing. "People are nuts."

"It's happened twice since I joined the fire department!" Cal grins and glances over at me in the passenger seat.

"I guess it's a blessing when it's just a toy car."

"Yeah, that's one way to look at it," he agrees, taking the Packer Avenue exit for the stadium.

"How long have you been a firefighter?"

"Six years. But I've always known I wanted to be a firefighter, ever since I was a kid. I love it, just like I bet you love teaching." He grins and I nod.

"Yeah, I've wanted to be a teacher since grade school. I'm so grateful I got a job in my field. I love my class, they're the greatest kids. I'm so lucky."

He flashes a smile my way and we continue talking about his job and mine, places we like to go in Philadelphia, that kind of thing. He mentions that he's on a fall softball league with the guys from his firehouse and tells me I should come watch him sometime. This date is going so well and Cal is nice. I mean, I might not feel butterflies with him exactly, but he's nice.

Cal pulls into the parking lot and we follow the slow trail of cars being directed to open spaces, filling in the rows of parking one after another. We finally come to an open space and pull in. Cal flips the visor down and grabs the game tickets, handing them to me before turning off the car.

We walk side by side towards the gate, still chatting. Yup, this date is perfect. The sun is shining, birds are chirping, clouds are in the sky, blah blah. I've totally got this dating thing.

We reach the gate and have our tickets scanned, then follow the directions towards our section, dodging people in the crowded venue. Cal grabs my hand and holds tight as we bob and weave, the smell of hot dogs and popcorn permeating the air while vendors walk around selling everything from team caps to beer. The closer we get the more I'm convinced we're going the wrong way. "Wow, are these really our seats? We're so close. Are these season tickets?" I stop, staring at the tickets in my hand to verify we're in the right place. We're on the fifty-yard line near the Eagles' bench. I think this is a better view than you get on TV.

"Yeah, got them from a friend." He grins as we find our seats and settle in. "I definitely owe him one, don't I?" he says with a wink.

We settle in and I check out the coaches and players standing what feels like feet away. They're running warm-up drills and we're so close I can hear the helmets crashing. I'm not that into football, but it's pretty cool to be this close. Around me the hum of the excited crowd escalates as the giant electronic screens count down the minutes until kickoff. I'm leaning all the way forward in my seat, taking it all in so that I have to turn my head back to see Cal. But he's not looking at the field, instead looking behind us.

"What's wrong?" I ask.

"Just looking for a hot dog guy. You want a hot dog?" he asks me, still glancing around.

"Sure, there's a guy right there." I point out the passing vendor, a guy dressed in stadium vendor clothing with one of those heated vending boxes strapped across his chest.

"Nah, let's have cheesesteaks instead. We're in Philly, right? I'll grab them and a couple beers. Be right back."

"Okay," I agree. If he wants cheesesteaks instead of a hot dog, what do I care? I return my focus to the field and pull my sleeves down, sticking my thumbs through the weird hole things in the seam. *It really is shaping up to be a perfect day,* I think as a breeze blows past and I reach to swipe the hair behind my ears.

Wait. Should I have gone with him? I'm so rude. I

should have gone with. I stand up and scoot my way down to the end of the aisle, apologizing to each person I have to slide in front of. Cal can't possibly carry all that by himself. And I should have offered to pay after he brought me here. No worries, I'll catch up with him in line. There's always a long line for food at the stadium.

I make my way up the stadium steps towards the main center walkway that leads to the interior side of the stadium where the food vendors are. It takes me a couple minutes to get there, dodging all the fans trying to reach their seats before the game starts. *I hope we don't miss kickoff,* I think regretfully as I glance back at one of the giant jumbotrons over the field counting down the minutes till game time. We don't have much time.

Once I reach the top of the steps and enter the concourse area I step to the side so I'm not blocking the walkway and glance around, trying to determine where Cal would have gone. I spot a Rita's Italian Ice and my mouth waters. I didn't know they had them here. *I wish I had time to grab one but I've got to find Cal first,* I think with one last glance at the Italian ice line. Okay, cheesesteaks... I see a place selling them a few feet away, but I don't see Cal in that line so I keep looking. I don't know why he'd have skipped this place, as it appears to be the closest one. Where the heck did he go? Wait, is that him over there? His back is to me. I can't tell. I take a step in that direction when I feel someone move too close to me in my peripheral vision.

"Miss? I'm going to need you to come with us."

It's stadium security.

Three

Chloe

"I don't understand," I say again as I'm led into some kind of conference room in the stadium. "Where's Cal? Is something wrong? What's going on?" Wait. Not a conference room. That sign said security office. I think this is a holding room of some sort. For criminals.

"Sit." The stadium officer points to a chair. There's a table with two chairs on one side and one on the other. There's even a surveillance window on the wall, like an episode of *Law & Order*. This has got to be a joke.

I sit. What else am I supposed to do? Make a run for it? I'm not a run-for-it kind of girl. Besides, I've done nothing wrong. I am not a criminal. I'm a second-grade teacher. Maybe something awful happened to Cal? Maybe he tripped and hit his head. Stadium seating involves a lot of stairs. Or maybe he got shanked while in line for a cheesesteak. With a plastic knife. It happens. I think I saw it once on TV. What if they need me to provide medical information? I don't know any medical information about Cal, I've met the guy twice.

I glance at the two-way mirror on the wall and wonder if someone is looking at me. I stuff my thumbs through the holes in the sleeves of my shirt and rest my folded elbows on the table in front of me and wait. And wait some more. Maybe they forgot about me? I wonder if I can just get up and leave? That would be rude though. Cal might need me. Unless he ditched me here, in which case I am not helping him.

The door opens and a man walks in. Not the stadium security who brought me here, someone new. He's in jeans and a gray long-sleeved t-shirt. The shirt is fitted. Fitted quite nicely, I can't help but notice. Dude's got some guns under that shirt. Guns? What the heck is wrong with me? I'm spending too much time with seven-year-olds.

He tosses a notepad onto the table and pushes the sleeves of his shirt up, revealing forearms lined with muscle. My eyes trail down and I note that he has nice hands. Smooth, even fingernails. Men too often overlook their fingernails. Bitten nails are the worst. He's got strong hands, I can tell. I'm certain if I were to shake his hand they would be dry and slightly calloused, but firm and strong.

I stop slouching on the table and sit up. He's... impressively good-looking. Picture every sexual fantasy you've ever had about a male model kind of good-looking. Only better, because he's not a twenty-year-old wearing skinny jeans. His hair is much like his nails, perfectly trimmed. Thick and dark. He's got a hint of a five o'clock shadow and I'm instantly curious what it would feel like under my fingertips.

"Special Agent Gallagher," he says, removing what looks like a wallet from his back pocket and flashing it at me as he takes a seat across from me. No, that's not a wallet, it's a badge. "Name?"

Wait. What just happened?

"You're a cop?" I spit out, stunned. I'm suddenly getting a sick feeling this has nothing to do with Cal choking on a cheesesteak.

"No, I'm a federal agent. Your name?" he repeats, pen poised over a notepad.

"Chloe Scott."

"Miss Scott, you have the tickets?" he asks, jotting my name down onto the pad. It's regular-sized. Not one of those tiny spiral ones that fit into a pocket like you see on TV. How will he get these notes back to his office? I'm not sure why this fascinates me in this moment, but it does.

I dig the tickets out of my pocket and slide them across the table, watching him as I do so. His eyes never leave me and it's making me nervous. And then I remind myself I probably should be nervous because I think I'm being questioned.

"Are you going to handcuff me?" I blurt. Why did I just ask him that? I don't even see any handcuffs.

"No." He tilts his head to the side, as if considering it. "Did you want me to?" he asks slowly, eyeing me. I can see a hint of a dimple in his cheek and the skin around his eyes creases as he stares at me. He's amused.

"No." I shake my head, eyes wide. Well, maybe a little bit. Not, like, right now or anything.

"Where did you get these tickets, Miss Scott?"

"I didn't get the tickets," I say, shaking my head. "I'm here with a date. My date got the tickets."

"Hmm." He runs his index finger across his bottom lip. They're nice lips. I hate that I have to note that at this moment, but it is what it is. He sits back and stares at me, silent. Why is he staring at me? I think he's trying to break me, like good cop-bad cop. Except it's just him. That, or he's thinking.

"I'll need to see your ID as well," he finally says.

"Um, sure." I unzip the tiny wristlet I brought to the

game. This stadium doesn't allow bags inside so I ditched my purse at home and brought this. Wait, I never put my ID in here. Cash, a credit card, my house key, phone and a Chapstick. *Don't panic, Chloe, I'm sure you won't be the only person who forgot their ID.* While being questioned by the Fed.

"I don't have it," I admit and try not to bite my lip.

He leans back in his chair and crosses his arms across his chest, watching me, eyes narrowed. "So you don't have any ID on you?"

"You know how they don't allow bags at this stadium," I say. "I threw my stuff in this"—I hold up my wristlet—"on the way out the door. It's not like much fits," I add, as I empty it out across the table. My key clatters against the metal table as the Chapstick hits the table and rolls towards him before I can grab it. He unfolds his arms and slaps a hand over it before it hits the edge. Then picks it up. I think he's going to hand it back, but instead he rolls it slowly between his fingers and examines it.

"Classic Strawberry," he reads from the label and then his gaze flicks to my lips. At least I think it does, it happens so fast. He rolls the tube again between his fingers before standing it up on the table in front of me so it won't roll.

"Thanks," I tell him. When he doesn't respond after a long pause I keep talking. "I don't understand what is happening," I say, shaking my head in confusion. "Am I in some kind of trouble? Where is Cal?"

"Who's Cal?" he asks, eyebrows raised in question. This seems to interest him.

"My date. I came here with him." I point my thumb behind me to indicate the stadium and I realize my thumb is still shoved through the stupid hole in the sleeve. I yank the sleeve lower and slide my thumb out. "Why am I here?" I ask, shaking my head. I'm starting to get frazzled now. "I am not a criminal. I'm a second-grade teacher on a really, really bad date. It didn't start that bad, I've had worse. But it's taken a definite turn into"—I blow out a breath—"lousy." I flop back into the folding chair and it squeaks for a moment before the room is silent.

"His name isn't Cal."

"I'm sorry, what?"

"The guy you came here with is not named Cal," he repeats.

I mull that over for a second. Maybe I should just cross 'learn how to date' off my to-do list without completing it.

"And if you didn't notice, he ditched you."

"Ditched me?"

"He saw stadium security headed towards him while you were still sitting in the stands. I assume he told you he was going to grab a beer and he'd be right back?"

I blow out a breath. "Not beer, cheesesteaks."

"How did you meet him?"

"Dating website."

"Yeah." He shakes his head. "You gotta be careful on those things."

"You think?" I retort.

He smiles at my sarcasm. "How long have you known him, Miss Scott?"

"This is our second date. I don't really know him that well. Obviously. He's a firefighter, said he got these tickets from a guy at work."

Agent Gallagher tilts his head at me, saying nothing.

Oh. "Not a firefighter either. Got it." I shake my head and avert my eyes to the ceiling for a second to collect myself. "So why am I here anyway? Are you investigating tragically bad dates?"

"The tickets," he says, tapping his index finger on the table next to the offending tickets, "are counterfeit." He pauses before continuing. "There's a lot more to it than that, but all I can tell you is that your date has been taken into custody."

I nod. I cannot catch a break. Also, this is humiliating. Why does this agent guy have to be so hot? I'm all flustered. If this happened to Everly she'd end up with a date. I'll be lucky not to end up in jail.

"Where'd he take you on the first date?" Agent Gallagher asks. He's tapping the pen against his lip, watching me.

"We met for coffee. I never let guys pick me up the first time I meet them. They could be criminals, you know?" I ask, then realize it's a stupid rhetorical question since I'm on a date with a criminal. Allegedly.

He nods. "Sure."

"So I met him at this great little coffee place. Really good coffee, by the way. Close to my apartment, but not too close. Super cute..." I trail off, frowning.

"What is it?"

"I met him at Mugshots. That coffee place on Fairmount? That's where we went for our first date. A place called Mugshots." I slap my palm against my forehead. "Fitting for my first date with a criminal. It's me. I attract weirdos. He seemed nice, you know?" I say, picking up steam. "You don't know what it's like out there. Cal seemed nice! He didn't even send me any POD's, which is more than I can say for most of the guys I meet online. I obviously have no business dating if I think the criminals seem nice. I've been watching crime TV for a decade and I've learned nothing. Nothing!"

"What's a POD?"

"Um…" Oh, shit. "Never mind," I say, waving my hand. "It's not important."

"Miss Scott," he says slowly, his face unreadable, his eyes intense. They're brown, but with all this depth. Flecks of gold and green that draw you in while still being enigmatic at the same time. I don't think I could lie to him, even if I had any talent at lying. "What is a POD?"

I blow out a huge breath and glance away. I am never repeating this story to Everly. "It's a dick pic." I dart a glance back to Agent Gallagher. "Guys send them all the time. It's so stupid." I roll my eyes. "I don't know why guys do that. Why do they do that?" I don't wait for a response. "My friend just started calling them POD's— Proof of Dick. She thinks it's classier or something, but I think she just wants to invent a new phrase. So yeah," I finish in a rush and shrug. "Sorry."

He stares at me for another moment, not saying anything, before he sits up and drags the notepad closer and starts writing again. He's probably making a note about dick pics in my file. Wait, do I have a file? I can't have a file, I'm a teacher, not a criminal. Anyway, I wish he would stop writing. No one needs a mention of POD's in his official report.

He asks me a few more questions, then tells me to sit tight while he verifies my information so he can release me.

Another half-hour later he returns and motions for me to follow him. "I think we're done here," he says. "Do you need help getting home?"

"No." I shake my head. "I'll catch a cab."

I'm not sure he's going to say anything else, but then he kinda smirks at me and says, "Be careful with the internet dating," before he walks away.

Um, thanks.

Four

Chloe

"Bye, Miss Scott!" The last of my students waves and bounds down the sidewalk to one of the buses idling at the curb. I wave back, a genuine smile on my face. These kids are the best part of my day, always.

I've known I wanted to be a teacher since I was a kid. School was my happy place, my constant no matter what was going on at home. My teachers supported me with kind words and patience and made me feel needed. I couldn't wait to grow up and be just like them.

I head back inside to straighten up my classroom before I head to the hospital. Sophie and Luke's daughter was born yesterday afternoon—Christine Caitlin Miller, weighing in at seven pounds, four ounces. Luke sent us a group text shortly after, a picture of a bundled Christine held by a beaming Sophie.

I sit at my desk and jot down notes from the day, reminders to myself on the kids who are struggling with one topic or another. I take notes where the children are excelling as well. Parent-teacher conferences will be here before I know it, and I want to have good feedback for each parent. But more than that, I want to ensure every child in my classroom is getting what they need from me.

An hour later I'm walking into Baldwin Memorial

Hospital, headed for the maternity floor. I know you're not supposed to like hospitals, but I always have. I think it's the activity. There are so many people in a hospital, like a small city filled with people working together to heal people. Some people might think sadness lingers in hospitals, but I've always thought the promise of hope is what lingers. People get fixed in hospitals. Bones set, wounds stitched. And brand-new human beings come into the world here, every single day.

I still can't believe Sophie's a mom. It doesn't feel like that long ago when we were all in college. I guess technically it *wasn't* that long ago, but it feels like Everly and Sophie are light years ahead of me. Not that it's a competition. It's not that. It's just the thought of putting myself out there again makes me kinda ill after yesterday's date.

I find Sophie in her room, glowing. Her light brown hair is pulled back in a low ponytail as she waves me into the room with a huge smile on her face. Baby Christine is perfect. I hold her, breathing in her perfect baby scent while she blinks at me and scrunches her face, then yawns. Everly arrives right behind me with her little guy Jake. He's wearing navy track pants, a white long-sleeved t-shirt and a navy tie. Everly is two-fisting paper cups from Grind Me, the coffee shop chain she worked at with Sophie during college.

"Still with the ties?" I whisper to Everly as she sets the cups down.

"It's a workday," she tells me and I try not to laugh. Jake turned five over the summer and started kindergarten this fall. He's a good kid, if a little serious.

"One decaf pumpkin spice latte," Everly announces, handing a cup to Sophie. "And a pumpkin muffin." She pulls a paper bag from her purse and sets it on the rolling tray over Sophie's bed.

"Ahh, this is heaven." Sophie moans in happiness as she pops a chunk of muffin into her mouth. "You would not believe how bad the food is here. I sent Luke home to take a shower and bring me something decent to eat."

"Well, I figured you could use a little pick-me-up from Grind Me. Just think, if it wasn't for their coffee you might never have met Luke and Christine might have never been conceived."

"What's conceived?" Jake asks from the couch. He's slumped back, feet dangling from the edge, listening to every word.

"It's how babies are made," Everly responds without missing a beat.

Jake slaps his palms over his eyes. "Okay. Stop." He asks if he can have Everly's phone and she slips it from her pocket and hands it to him as she snatches Christine from me. I scoot over next to Jake.

"Whatcha playing?" I ask him as he taps the screen.

"I'm catching Pokemon," he tells me, looking up.

"Me too!" I tell him, pulling out my phone and opening the app. "I'm not very good at it though. I don't have very many yet, but I got this cute purple mouse." I hold up my phone to show him.

"Auntie Chloe." He shakes his head at me. "That's a rat. You can catch them anywhere." This kid. He calls us all Auntie even though none of us are technically his aunts. It's pretty cute though, and I'm ecstatic to be an honorary aunt.

"Humph, maybe we should go for a walk and see if we can catch something better? I think there's a Pokestop in the lobby."

"Yeah!" His face lights up. "Mom! Auntie Chloe and I are gonna go catch Pokemon," he announces. Everly tells us to have fun and off we go.

You have to walk to make this game work, so we investigate the hospital, walking to the cafeteria, the lobby, the chapel, the gift shop and the coffee shop. Jake tells me all about kindergarten, his teacher and his new friends at school and his cat. He catches a ton of Pokemon before we head back upstairs. An elevator opens just as I'm trying to nab another Pokemon. We step on while I fling virtual balls at a pigeon. I hold the phone in front of me, tilting the screen and my body like it's going to help me nab the thing.

"Did you get it yet?" Jake asks.

"No." I bend my knees so he can see the screen too, continuing to hold the phone in front of me with one hand and using the other to swipe the screen, flinging virtual balls. I bite my lip as I lob the next ball. I think I've got 'em this time, but a man clearing his throat catches my attention before I can be sure. I glance up, knees still bent as I crouch next to Jake, phone extended in my hand... and realize that at this angle my extended hand is inches from... oh, my God, this guy probably thinks I'm trying to take a picture of his dick. I mean, I can kinda see the outline of it, right—no, stop. I shoot up, an apology on my lips before I'm fully standing.

"I'm so sorry! We're playing this game..." I wave the phone in my hand as I say it, but then my eyes land on his and the phone is slipping out of my hand.

It's the hot agent from yesterday. Only today he's wearing a suit. A nice one. Why don't men dress like this anymore? Clearly he's a man, and he's dressed like this. I mean the other men. The men whom I come in contact with on a regular basis. They don't look like this.

Quickly, I bend my knees and scoop my phone off the floor where it's landed next to his shoe. Dammit, he has nice shoes too. This is so embarrassing. *Get it together, Chloe.*

"There was a Pikachu on your pants," I say, referring to the Pokemon game I was playing as I stand again and my head jerks and I stumble towards him. Oh, Jesus. A strand of my hair is wrapped around the button on his jacket. How? How does this happen to me? I reach forward to free myself when his hand moves forward and grips my forearm.

"Stop," he says, his tone firm. "Hold still," he adds, and I blow out a breath and still myself. His hand leaves my arm and he untangles my hair from the button as the elevator stops. Once free I stand, sure I'm beet red. I dart a quick glance at the man. His perfect, beautiful face is now showing a hint of amusement.

I realize the elevator is stopped so I turn to see what floor we're on and realize Everly is standing in the hallway holding the elevator door open with a smug smile on her face. She reaches out a hand to Jake as we all step off the elevator. "I see that you two met?" she questions with... is that glee on her face?

Wait. Oh, shit. The badge. This must be...

"No." I shake my head back and forth. "Nope, I've never seen this guy before," I lie. I will never hear the end of it from Everly if she finds out I've already met Sophie's brother—while he was arresting my date. Just no.

"Ahh, Everly," the man says. "It's been a while." He slides his hands in his pockets and glances between the two of us and Jake, seeming to realize something. "This little guy must belong to you," he says, nodding at Jake. "My sister mentioned you got married"—he pauses—"and you're a mom now," he adds, looking at Jake as if the notion that Everly is partially responsible for raising

33

someone is a confusing thought. He's not wrong, it is bizarre.

Everly nods. "This is Jake. And this is Chloe," she adds, nodding towards me, with a big smile on her face. Big. When she turns back towards Boyd I shake my head, eyes wide. I hope he plays along.

"Chloe." He says it slowly, as if testing the name out, running his eyes over me even slower. Apparently he's got all the time in the world. I fidget under his gaze before he speaks. "No, we haven't met."

"Chloe was my roommate in college," she tells him before turning to me. "This is Boyd Gallagher, Sophie's brother." She smiles, before adding, "The Fed."

Right. Way to be obvious, Everly. Why didn't I put this together yesterday? Because I didn't recognize the name Gallagher. Obviously he has a different last name than Sophie did before she got married, it just never occurred to me to think about it until now. I swallow and stick my hand out. "Nice to meet you."

He pauses for a fraction of a second, his bottom lip tugged between his teeth, before he removes his right hand from his pocket and reaches forward to shake mine. His hand is firm and rougher than my own, and I catch a whiff of his aftershave as our hands connect. He holds onto my hand a moment longer than necessary and I like it, but it makes me panic at the same time.

"Sorry about the elevator," I say, backing up a foot. I need space before I do or say anything else embarrassing. He looks even better than he did yesterday. Stupid suit. He's easily over six feet, broad shoulders, narrow waist. His tie lies flat down his abdomen over what must be perfect abs.

He doesn't say anything, just trails his eyes over me.

"Pokemon!" I blurt out when I can't take the silence.

See? I'm such an idiot. "Um, okay then," I add in for good measure and cross my arms across my chest and look at my scuffed shoes. I'm wearing leggings covered in a donut print. Jesus, no wonder he was looking me over. These freaking leggings are all the rage at my school, all the teachers are wearing them. I normally stick to the plain black ones or a modest print, but no, I let one of the other teachers talk me into these during a pop-up sale. "The kids will love them," she told me. "You can pair it with a cute denim jacket," she said. I'm burning these the second I get home. No wonder I can't get laid.

"I was just coming to look for you," Everly says, interrupting my thoughts. "We're going to take off. I have to get home and make Sawyer's dinner," she deadpans then laughs. "I'm totally kidding. I just wanted to hear what that sounded like coming out of my mouth. Jake does have soccer though, so we have to go. You can show Boyd where Sophie's room is," Everly states as she jabs the elevator button.

"Um, yeah." I glance towards Boyd then give Jake a high-five. "Thanks for helping me catch the Pokemon, buddy." And then they're gone and I'm left with Mr. Hottie.

I really need to go home and take off my pants.

Instead I nod to Boyd to follow me towards Sophie's room. Her room is only a few doors down from the elevator, but it feels like a really long walk with Boyd behind me. His shoes click against the linoleum floor while mine make the occasional squeak. Am I breathing weirdly? I think I'm breathing weirdly. I wonder how ridiculous these leggings look from behind. I remind myself to look in the mirror when I get home just so I have a clear mental image of this moment to torment myself with.

"Is this going to be our thing now?" he asks.

"Donuts?" I ask, confused, glancing at him behind me.

His eyes move to my leggings-covered ass and he laughs. "No, awkward meetings."

"Why are you dressed like that?" I blurt out, then slap my hand over my mouth.

"Excuse me?" he replies, brows raised.

"Nothing."

"No, I think you had a question about my clothing?" he says, glancing down at his suit and then back to me. He takes a moment to run his eyes over my donut leggings before meeting my eyes.

"I teach the second grade!" I protest, in defense.

"I catch criminals," he retorts. "What's wrong with my suit?"

"The federal government cannot be paying you enough to dress like James Bond."

"So you like the way I look," he clarifies with a confident smirk.

"Obviously," I say, then catch myself and add a sarcastic, "Not," to the end. What is wrong with me? Why am I behaving like a bitch? If I had any idea what I was doing with men I'd be doing it right now, not insulting him. I pause in front of Sophie's door and turn to him. "Thank you for going along with me back there," I say, referring to my fib to Everly about not having met him previously. "I love Everly, but she's a little..." I trail off.

"Nuts. The girl is nuts," he says. "But it's fine. Now you owe me a favor," he adds with a little lift to his eyebrow, then pushes open the door to Sophie's room. I follow him in, confused about what kind of favor he could want from me, but I don't have time to think about it too hard.

"Boyd!" Sophie calls, as we walk into the room. "I'm so glad you could make it. Thank you for the flowers."

The baby is back in the weird plastic hospital bassinet and she lets out a little cry, calling our attention to her.

"I'll get her," I tell Sophie when it looks like she might get out of bed to grab her. "No one should have to get up in one of those hospital gowns," I add. I calm her and then Sophie insists Boyd should hold his niece.

"I'm good, thanks." He nods from his position by the window.

"You'll hold her," I snip. "She's only going to be a day old once."

I realize this is a mistake as soon as I'm in front of him with the baby. Not because he's not capable, no. He takes the baby with ease. Not because standing this close I now know how good he smells. And not because I now know how freaking firm his chest is against my arm as I gently pass Christine to him. No, all of those things I could handle. It's the brush of his fingertips against my breast—completely innocent—as the baby is passed from me to him. The brush of fingertips that instantly makes both nipples hard. He didn't even touch both of them. Is that normal? Are they supposed to get hard together? I mentally add this to my list of things I need to Google as I cross my arms across my chest and step away from him.

He shoots me a smile that makes me suspect he knows exactly how uncomfortable he makes me before turning his attention to the baby in his arms. I grab my jacket and congratulate Sophie again and let her know I'll stop by this week once she's home. Then I book it outta there.

Five

Chloe

The next couple of days pass in the usual blur of lesson plans, notes to parents, and breaking up the bickering of seven-year-olds. I love it. I might be almost as new to teaching as I am to dating, but unlike dating, I'm good at teaching. Plus I've worked hard to prepare myself to be a great teacher. Which, now that I'm thinking of it like that, reminds me that I just need more practice with dating. It's not like I gave up the first time a kid was difficult. Nope. Maybe I should study? Like a course, or a book. I wonder if there's a *Dating for Dummies* book? I'm going to Google that right now... there is! Um, look, there's a *Sex for Dummies* too. I bite my lip, then add them both to my online cart and check out. I'm a great student. I've totally got this.

My books will be here in a couple of days. In the meantime, I've got another date tonight. Another chance to practice, if you will. Like homework. I'm just meeting the guy for coffee—that's my go-to first date. I need to stop at home first and freshen up. One time I met someone after work and didn't realize until later that I had a streak of blue Sharpie down my arm the entire time. So I pack up and drive home first to get ready.

I'm meeting Joe at a Starbucks near my apartment, the

one on South Broad Street. It's not the closest coffee shop to my apartment—not even the closest Starbucks. I never meet dates super close to my apartment, just in case. Like, what if it's a horrible date and I keep bumping into them at my favorite Starbucks? That would be awful. Plus the employees would see me in there all the time with different guys. So embarrassing.

Luckily I can leave school early enough to avoid some of the rush-hour traffic, so I make it home in under twenty minutes. Teacher perk. I park my car for the night in the cheap monthly parking garage I found a couple of blocks from my apartment. I don't live anywhere fancy enough to include parking. The location is amazing though. I'm downtown in Center City, Philadelphia, only a few blocks away from Sophie and less than ten blocks from both Sandra and Everly. But I live in a small studio apartment. One-bedrooms were way out of my price range if I wanted to be downtown. So I don't have fancy amenities like parking or in-unit laundry, or a doorman. But it's a secure building with a great location and it's really all I need.

I'm on the eighth floor, which makes for a nice view and somewhat reduced noise coming from the street. I walk inside and drop the bag I bring to school with me on one of the chairs at my small two-seat kitchen table and shrug out of my jacket. I stuff today's clothes into my hamper then change into jeans and a black sweater before checking my hair and makeup. My hair is kind of a sandy brown with streaks of auburn and right now, it's a mess. A glance at the clock tells me I don't have time to do much with it, so I brush it out and fasten it in a low pony. It will have to do. I apply a little more makeup than I wear to school then freshen my Chapstick before applying a nude lipstick on top. Perfect. I check my phone to make sure he hasn't cancelled then grab my purse and jacket and head out.

I'll walk to Starbucks. It's less than a mile and it's nice out. I cut through Rittenhouse Square to 18th Street, then walk a few blocks down before turning and making my way towards South Broad. I'm a little apprehensive after my date last weekend, but I Googled this guy and I'm reasonably sure he's a real person. I found some pictures online that match the pictures on his dating profile, so assuming the guy in the pictures is the guy who shows up, I should be okay.

But this is why I always meet first dates in a public place. I let Cal pick me up on the second date, but I didn't let him come upstairs. I met him in the lobby. I live in a large building so I figure it's okay to meet them in the lobby for the second date. I haven't actually let anyone into my apartment yet. I should probably stop watching *Criminal Minds* if I want to get a boyfriend. It's just so good. But I think it might be making me paranoid. I mean, the agents on *Criminal Minds* catch at least twenty new serial killers every season. There can't possibly be that many serial killers wandering around, right? There's probably like... ten in the United States at any given time. I bet it's ten. I'm gonna look that up later.

I wonder what Boyd meant about me owing him a favor. I wonder if he meant anything by it? I wonder what I want him to mean. I stuff my hands into my pockets as I walk. Like, what if he meant a sexual favor? No, that's stupid. Stupid. As if he'd need a sexual favor from me. He probably meant a favor like helping him move. I wrinkle my nose and step around a couple arguing in the middle of the sidewalk. Or maybe a favor like a ride to the airport. That's probably what he meant. I can't really picture him sitting in the passenger seat of my

Toyota Corolla though, even for a free ride to the airport.

I roll my eyes at myself as I walk. I'm sure he meant nothing by it. It's just a stupid saying. It does not, in any way, imply that he was thinking dirty thoughts about me. As if he would look twice at me anyway. I'm cute enough, I suppose. But that's the thing. I'm cute. I get freckles in the summer. I wear leggings and I'm happy with my hair in a ponytail. He seems like he'd appreciate someone a little more... polished than me. Plus, he's older. I seem to recall that he's ten years older than Sophie, which would make him thirty-two and way more experienced than me. Forget about it. But maybe I should increase my age limit on the dating app I'm using. I think I have it capped at twenty-eight. Maybe I should raise it because I think thirty-two-year-olds might be my thing. You know, as long as they have badges and look like Boyd.

I blow out a breath and tap my foot on the pavement while I wait for the light to change so I can cross 15th Street. What would I even do with a guy like Boyd? He's probably into crazy shit like having sex with the lights on. It's just... I swear I felt something when we met. The moment he walked into the room on Sunday the energy changed. Granted I was about to be questioned by the FBI, so that might have had something to do with the energy in the room, but I don't know. The problem with chemistry is that it's not always reciprocated. Sometimes one person is picturing Hollywood-worthy wall sex and the other person is thinking about what they should pick up for dinner on the way home from work.

It's likely it will be months before I see him again anyway, owed favor or not. I managed to go almost a year without meeting him the first time. He met Sophie for the first time last fall after discovering she was his half-sister, and Everly's crossed paths with him, but I hadn't until Sunday. So there's no reason I will again. *Just put him out of your head, Chloe. He's way too much for you anyway.* Everly would know what to do with a guy like that. Me, not so much.

I make it to the Starbucks on Broad with a little under ten minutes to spare, so I get in line to order. I like to avoid the awkward who-is-going-to-pay shuffle at the counter and scope out a good table and I've got just enough time to do both. I order the seasonal pumpkin spice latte in decaf then nab an empty two-seat table with a good view of the door so I can keep an eye out for Joe. He arrives a couple of minutes later and scans the cafe for me and when his gaze lands on me I confirm with a small wave. He nods with a small smile and heads my way.

"Can I get anything else for you?" he asks, nodding at the cup in my hands as he removes his coat and places it over the back of the chair across from mine.

"No, thank you. I'm good with this," I say, lifting the paper cup an inch off the table. "Go grab something for yourself," I tell him with a smile. Luckily there's no line so he's back shortly, drink in hand.

"So, Chloe, it's nice to meet you," he says as he takes a seat.

"You as well," I return. "Thanks for meeting me here."

"No problem. I live in the Washington Square area so this wasn't too far for me." He takes a sip from his cup then continues when I don't say anything. "I've enjoyed chatting with you online. I'm glad we were finally able to meet."

"I'm just happy you match your photos," I say, then try not to visibly cringe. What a stupid thing to say. He's really cute. And nice. And I'm my usual nervous awkward self. But he just laughs like it's no big deal.

"Were you worried I was a forty-year-old guy using old photos?" he asks with a wide smile, clearly trying to put me at ease.

"No, no. I'm sorry, that was rude. It's just that I went out last weekend with a guy who gave me a fake name *and* got arrested on our date," I babble, trying to explain. Why did I just say that? That's worse. I shouldn't have said that, I'm pretty sure it's bad form to bring it up.

"Um, wow," he responds, the smile slipping just a little.

"I'm not usually that bad at picking them," I reveal, then wish I could suck it back in. *Shut up, Chloe!*

"So, you're a teacher?" he asks after a moment, clearly throwing me a lifeline and trying to redirect the conversation.

"Yeah," I say, thankful for the switch in topics and happy that he's obviously better at this than I am. "Second grade," I add, my voice trailing off as I catch something over Joe's shoulder.

Boyd Gallagher.

He's got a cup in hand and he's striding towards the exit when he turns his head and his eyes land on mine. I see the flicker of surprise cross his face as I turn my attention back to Joe.

"Second grade," I repeat. "I teach second grade. I love it."

Joe nods. "My mom's a teacher, so I know how hard you work."

I'm focusing on Joe but I see Boyd approaching from the corner of my eye. Is he going to interrupt my date to say hi? So awkward.

But he doesn't.

No.

Instead, he takes a seat at the table next to ours. In the seat next to Joe so he's facing me. And then he ignores me.

He's... pretending he doesn't know me? Seriously? I dart another glance in his direction but he's not looking at me. He's set his coffee on the table and is doing something with his phone. His posture is relaxed as if he's intending to stay a while. What the heck is he doing? I know he saw me. I know he did. A fact confirmed when he meets my gaze dead on the next time I glance in his direction, a brow raised in amusement. He's in another fancy suit today. It's black and the white shirt he's wearing underneath it looks crisp and fresh, even though this must be the end of his day as well. He's wearing a charcoal tie which he straightens, his fingers running down the midsection of the tie, smoothing the material as he takes a sip from his cup.

"Is everything okay?" Joe asks.

"Yes!" I agree quickly. "I was just checking out the light fixtures," I say, nodding to the Starbucks decor. "They're nice, don't you think?" Not a total lie. I've always appreciated the ambiance here. "They must have them custom-made," I muse. *Brilliant conversational skills, Chloe.*

"I guess." Joe shrugs.

"I mean, it's not like you can buy them just anywhere," I add, because I never quit when I should.

"I imagine not," he agrees. "They don't want just anyone to get their hands on their exclusive light fixtures." He says it kindly, like he's not bothered by my inane light fixture observations.

"Right." I nod. Joe is really so nice. And he's really good-looking. He's got beautiful thick dark hair. "Are you Italian?"

"No." He shakes his head. "Well, I don't think so. I'm adopted so I've got no idea. My parents are of Scottish and German descent."

Oh. "I love Italian food," I respond. Because that's an appropriate response to sticking your foot in your mouth.

"I hate Italian." Joe frowns and shakes his head, then laughs. "Just kidding. Who doesn't love Italian food?"

Why is Boyd watching? Is this some sort of payback for pretending not to know him the other day at the hospital? I'm sure I can't be the only girl questioned by the FBI who didn't want her friends to know about it. Sheesh. Oh, my God. Is he on a stakeout? Is he investigating this date too? No. I mentally shake my head. Not possible.

"Have you ever been to Serafina? On 18th? My friend went into labor there last week."

"Um, wow. Okay." He pauses. "Congratulations to your friend," he adds slowly, because he's probably unsure what the correct response is to that tidbit of information.

"I'm sorry," I say, waving my hand. "I meant to say, they have great Italian food there. My friend did go into labor at lunch, but you probably didn't need to know that part."

"No, it's fine. I'm sure that was a pretty exciting lunch."

"Yeah." We sit in silence for a moment and then, "Hey, do you want to hear a joke?" *Say no. Stop speaking, Chloe.*

"Sure."

"Why did the banana go to the doctor?" Yup. I'm telling second-grade jokes.

"Why?"

"Because it wasn't peeling well!"

Joe nods and does a fake laugh. So I continue, like an idiot. "Wait, I've got a better one," I blurt out. "Why did the jellybean go to school?"

"Why?"

"He wanted to become a Smartie!"

I wish I could say I stopped here. But I think I told at least two more before Joe finally gave up and politely checked his watch. I don't think I'm ready for dating. The single men of Philadelphia should not be subjected to the disaster that is me. And Boyd watching did not help.

"Okay, well, thanks!" I say, shooting to my feet and sticking my hand out like I just completed a job interview, not a date. Yeah. I imagine it's going to be a solid decade before I can erase this memory from my mind.

His eyes widen a bit in surprise but, ever the gentleman, he quickly recovers and shakes my hand, wishing me a good night. Then he bolts out of there. I watch as the glass door swings open and he retreats from view before I turn to Boyd. He's smiling.

SIX
BOYD

"What are you doing?" she asks me, head tilted to the side, her brows raised in question. She's fighting to keep her face neutral but her eyes are slightly narrowed, telling me that she's likely annoyed with me—as she should be—but waiting to hear my answer before she commits to it. Her ponytail dangles to the side with the tilt of her head and while I don't think I've ever been a fan of ponytails previously, I am now.

"You're kind of a disaster," I respond. That's not really an answer, more of an observation.

"No." She shakes her head and narrows her eyes further, her tone most certainly moving towards annoyed. "Why are you here? At that table specifically? Watching me?"

"I saw you and I was curious." That's true. I was halfway to the door when I spotted her. On her date. Nice guy too. I gotta give him credit for sticking it out as long as he did. Not too much credit, because look at her. You'd have to be an idiot not to try.

"Curious? Are you serious?" Her eyes widen. Yup. Definitely annoyed. "You are such a dick!" She drops her voice to a whisper when she says dick and I know it's because it offends her schoolteacher sensibilities to swear in public. But hearing her whisper it combined with a quick glance around to make sure no one is listening to her, well, that shit is downright erotic.

"Fascinated," I confirm with a slight nod. "I mean, when you started in with the knock-knock jokes, wow."

She levels me with a glare that might keep schoolchildren in line but can't be very effective with grown men.

"I don't…" She stalls. "I'm not very good at dating."

"You could use some help," I agree. And I am feeling uncharacteristically helpful.

"I just…" She glances at me and then away again. "I get nervous and then I panic and act weird. I'm pretty normal most of the time. When I'm by myself." She shrugs then folds her arms across her chest and wrinkles her nose at me. "You're around an awful lot lately. Are you stalking me?"

"Stalking you? This is *my* Starbucks. I live around the corner," I tell her. "There's at least two Starbuckses closer to your apartment than this one. I think you picked *this* Starbucks so you'd run into me." I can't imagine that's true, but I wouldn't mind it if it was. She's been on my mind since I first laid eyes on her almost a week ago.

"Uh, no," she replies sarcastically. It seems to be her go-to when she's nervous. "I never meet first dates anywhere within a three-block radius of my apartment."

A three-block radius? She kills me. She cannot be getting laid much, which pleases me in some ridiculously caveman way.

"Well, that sounds very… safe of you."

She nods in a way that tells me she's a little bit smug about her safety rules. She's so fucking cute. She was cute in the holding room at the stadium too. I didn't actually need to question her that day; I was going to send her packing as soon as I walked into the room, but… I just wanted to hear her talk. I saw her through the two-way surveillance mirror fidgeting on the uncomfortable metal folding chair. She was bouncing one sneaker-clad foot on the ground and twirling the end of a strand of hair around her fingers. I was intrigued by her. I'm not sure why exactly, but I was drawn to her. I'd already pulled her information before I walked into the room, so I knew she was a twenty-two-year-old recent graduate, currently employed at an elementary school. Not my type.

Then she'd asked if I was going to handcuff her. Jesus. The visual of her handcuffed—to my bed—had materialized in my head in a heartbeat.

"So Joe, he's some guy you met on the internet?" I ask her, tapping my fingers against the table.

"Yeah." She sighs and glances back at the door. "He was nice, right? I totally blew that."

Yes, she did. Thank fuck.

"I'm ready for my favor now," I tell her as my course of action becomes clear, but she's shaking her head before I've finished speaking.

"I don't think you deserve a favor anymore," she responds, back straight and chin tilted up. Her ponytail bounces with the shake of her head and she crosses her arms across her chest for emphasis. "After spying on me, you spier!" She pauses a second then, softening, asks, "You're not an actual spy, right?"

"No." I shake my head slowly back and forth. This girl. I sit back in my chair and wait a beat before I respond further. "Okay then. If you're okay with my sister and Everly knowing you almost got arrested—"

"I didn't get arrested!" she interrupts in a not-whisper as her eyes flare in outrage. She slides into the chair across from mine and lowers her voice. "I did not get arrested. I was simply detained for a couple of hours," she says with a little shake of her head, trying to play it off as no big deal when I know damn well it totally freaked her out.

"Still." I shrug. "Such an entertaining story…" I trail off. I'm not going to have to push this very hard. She's putting up a token fight, but she's curious about me and she's got to at least want to find out what my request is.

"Shouldn't I be protected by agent-suspect confidentiality?"

"You mean something like doctor-patient privilege?" I ask her. "Or lawyer-client?"

"Yeah." She nods. "Exactly."

"Nope." I shake my head. "Sorry."

"So what do you want?" she asks, shoulders hunched and her gaze suspicious.

"I need a date to a wedding next weekend."

The tension drops from her shoulders and her suspicion is replaced with confusion. "Like you can't get a real date?" It comes out kinda snarky and exasperated and makes me want to grin.

"I could, but they're so much work." I drag my hand over my jaw as if I'm seriously contemplating this. "If I bring a real date she'll read into it and think I brought her so I can introduce her to my family. And if I go alone my mother will ensure I'm sat next to some horrible woman she's picked out for me."

"But why would you want me to go with you? I'm a disaster, as you so eloquently put it. Won't I embarrass you?" She bites her lip and stares at me, eyes wide.

"Since it's not a real date I assume you won't be nervous and thus less disastrous," I answer. "Unless I make you nervous?" I add slowly, with a slight frown, as if the idea has just occurred to me. It hasn't. I know I make her nervous and it probably makes me an asshole, but I like it. "Besides, it'll be good practice for you."

"Practice?"

"Your abominable dating skills," I remind her, shifting my eyes to the empty table beside us, recently vacated by Joe. "We can work on appropriate conversations you should be having with an adult male." As long as that adult male is me.

She bites on her bottom lip and stares at me for a moment, thinking. I can wait because I already know what her answer is going to be. I pick at a piece of lint on the sleeve of my suit coat and straighten the cuffs. Finally she nods. "Okay," she says. "I guess I do owe you," she adds, then rolls her eyes in my face and sighs. I nod, keeping my smile to myself.

"You'll need a dress," I tell her and wait for the objection I know is coming.

"I have dresses," she replies, but tiny lines of concern mar her forehead and I've been with enough women to know what's going through her head. Does she have the right dress for this? How fancy is the event? What will everyone else be wearing? Add to that—she can't have the budget for a dress. She's fresh out of college and on a teacher's salary, both of which tell me it isn't likely she has an appropriate dress hanging in her closet. *Shit, this entire scheme is pure genius,* I think, as I make a mental note to cancel the date I had lined up for this wedding when I get home.

"This is a formal event. We'll pick up a dress this weekend."

She gives me a dirty look. "What do you mean we'll pick up a dress this weekend?"

"I mean shopping. I'll pick you up at ten on Saturday."

"I can find a dress by myself," she says firmly.

"Please. You were wearing pants with donuts on them

the second time I saw you. If you can even call those things pants." Fucking leggings left nothing to the imagination. And I've done a lot of imagining. Mostly involving her legs wrapped around my hips. "Half my family is going to be there. I'll pick out the dress." I could give a fuck about the dress. I want to spend time with her that she thinks isn't a date, so she'll relax and be herself.

"Well, that was rude," she deadpans.

I shrug. "Besides, you're doing me a favor," I remind her, "so the dress is on me."

"Whatever," she agrees sullenly.

"You're welcome," I reply.

"You're impossible," she says with a shake of her head. "I should go," she adds a moment later with a glance towards the window. "It's getting late."

I walk her outside and she stops, standing on one foot and tapping the toe of her other on the sidewalk. "Well, bye," she says and turns to walk away.

"You walked here?" I ask, stopping her.

"Of course, it's less than a mile."

"Well, you're not walking home," I inform her while simultaneously flagging a cab.

"Boyd, the sidewalks are well occupied the entire route back to my apartment and it's before ten. Perfectly safe."

A cab stops and I open the back door for her while passing the driver enough cash to cover her fare home. "Oh, no, safety girl, I can't let you walk home after that story about how you walked all the way over here because you don't meet dates within a three-block radius of your apartment," I tell her with a lazy grin while resting my arm across the top of the open cab door. "I feel a male responsibility to ensure you get home safe after that fascinating tidbit."

"You're a jerk," she tells me. But she gets in the cab and I smile. This girl isn't going to be easy.

Seven

Chloe

Boyd Gallagher is... something. I'm not sure what, exactly. But he's something. He thinks I'm awkward, but at least I've never crashed someone's date. Or sat silently and watched. Or whatever he was doing. I suppose he gets away with whatever he wants because he's good-looking; no one's ever had the nerve to tell him that his behavior is strange.

I can't believe I have to go to a wedding with him, but he's right, I do owe him and I do need the practice. And that thought brings another horrifying thought to mind— what if there's dancing at the wedding? No, not what if, of course there will be dancing at the wedding. He said it's formal, what formal wedding doesn't have dancing? None that I've ever heard of. I don't know how to dance, not really. I haven't been to a dance since high school and no one had any idea what they were doing at those dances. When a slow song came on you just shuffled back and forth with your date until the song ended.

I feel the familiar swell of panic rise and then I tamp it back down. It's not a real date. If Boyd wants to dance at this wedding I'll just tell him I don't know what I'm doing and he'll guide me through it. He might laugh at me, but who cares? It's not like I'm trying to impress a fake date. Crisis averted, relax.

My class is at lunch which means I'm at lunch. Thirty-five minutes of quiet time. Otherwise known as thirty-five minutes of me sitting by myself in the teachers' lounge. You grow up thinking lunch trauma will end with high school. It doesn't.

I'm new. I get it. But school started six weeks ago and teacher in-service two weeks before that. So I'm not *that* new. Not as new as the substitute who replaced Mrs. Clark when she left on maternity leave three weeks into the school year. The substitute who went to see that new suspense movie everyone is talking about with Mrs. Hildrew last weekend. And knits with Miss Ackerley on Tuesdays. Apparently that's a thing. Knitting Tuesdays. And fine, I don't knit, but how is it so *easy* for her to fit in?

Making new friends is hard. Everly has been my best friend since forever. She's always been there—next store, at school, in college. People gravitate towards her and I benefited from that. Because truthfully, Everly is my friend pimp. She's the one who brought Sophie and Sandra into my life. She's the one who organized our trick-or-treating posse in grade school. Brought the guys around in high school and made friends with every girl on our floor in college.

And now she's gone. Fine. That might be overly dramatic. She's not gone, she's married. But for the first time in my entire life, Everly is living more than five hundred yards away. She's living one mile away, if you're counting. I could walk there in under twenty minutes. But it's different. We're not living in the same tiny dorm room anymore.

I just didn't realize the transition to adulthood would be so lonely. Which is silly, but how can you really know what it's going to feel like ahead of time? And I had no idea it would so hard to make friends at work. We're teachers, for crying out loud. Elementary school teachers. I just gotta keep trying, that's what I remind myself. And what I'd tell my students. I should walk the walk, right?

So when I enter the teachers' lounge and see that I have two options—an empty table, and an empty seat at a table with a few other teachers—I plop myself down at their table. And say hello, even though I'm shaking inside because I'm so nervous. Nervous I'll trip over my words and sound stupid. Or choke on a bread crumb and draw attention to myself. Or just be inadequate in some way. You get the idea.

But it goes okay, I think. Not great, but okay. These women are firmly entrenched in their friendship routines. They don't need a newbie, so they're apathetic. Still, I try. So when Miss Michaels mentions that she's dying to try out the new coffee shop in Center City and I ask if she'd like to meet there on Sunday, I try not to take it personally when she shrugs and says she doesn't really like to leave the house on the weekends.

Okay then.

I can always go by myself. Again.

After work I park my car in the garage and then walk over to Sophie's. Her condo is super close to my apartment, which is a huge bonus. My studio apartment would fit into the nursery of her fancy penthouse apartment, but it's worth living in a small space to be in a great location so it's fine with me.

Her husband Luke greets me at the door, a burp cloth slung over his shoulder and a huge smile on his face. He takes me back to the den connected to the kitchen, where Sophie's sitting on the couch with baby Christine swaddled up in a blanket lying on the cushion next to her.

"Can I hold her?" I question after giving Sophie a hug.

"Of course!" She beams and places the baby in my arms. "I was just staring at her for a bit."

"Staring at her?" I question. I'm not sure why, because now I'm staring at her. I brush a fingertip across her head while she blinks at me. She's so stinking cute.

"Yeah, I think I'm holding her too much. Like all the time. Do you think all the time's too much?" Sophie frets from the sofa. I'm sitting diagonal to her on a cushy chair and I settle back and snuggle the baby closer.

"I think she's five days old so it's probably okay to hold her as much as you want."

Sophie nods. "That's what Luke said, but I thought maybe he was just being nice."

"She smells so yummy," I comment.

"Right?" Sophie exclaims. "I thought maybe it was just me since I'm a little biased but she does smell delicious, doesn't she? Like baby powder and peaches."

"Exactly like that. So how are you feeling?"

"Like I gave birth less than a week ago, but otherwise good," she jokes.

"You look great," I assure her. And she does. She's glowing and I think motherhood is going to suit her just fine.

"She's an easy baby so far, plus Luke seems to know what he's doing so that helps my confidence, you know?"

I nod.

"So what are you up to this weekend? Anything fun?" she asks.

Shoot. Am I supposed to tell her that I'm dress-shopping with Boyd? Because I'm attending a wedding with him next weekend? Because I owe him a favor for keeping quiet about my date getting arrested? No. Definitely not. There's no way I want to bring any of that up, so I focus on the baby instead and mutter something about working on lesson plans. It's not a total lie. I'll work on lesson plans as well as go shopping with her brother.

"So what did you think of Boyd?"

"What?" My head snaps up from the baby and I glance at Sophie. Am I that bad a liar?

"Boyd? My brother? You met him at the hospital on Monday?"

Oh, okay, whew. "He seemed nice," I offer. I'm not sure why. 'Nice' isn't really at the top of my descriptive words for Boyd Gallagher. Words like 'gorgeous,' 'cocky,' 'nosy,' 'fit,' 'sophisticated,' 'chiseled' and 'resourceful' come to mind. But 'nice' works too.

"Everly seems to think the two of you would be good together," she says, trying to dig into my thoughts on the subject.

"Yes, well, Everly also spent fifteen years thinking she and Finn Camden were a perfect match. You can't always believe her."

"True enough," Sophie agrees with a laugh.

EIGHT
BOYD

At ten minutes to ten I knock on Chloe's apartment door. I know I'm early, but I also know that in another five minutes she'll be waiting for me in the lobby. I'm sure I'm breaching some safety rule of hers by coming to her door, but fuck it. I want to see where she lives.

The door flings open a moment later and she's shaking her head and throwing her hands up. "You're early," she says, leaving the door open and pivoting around. Fucking hell. She's got another pair of those goddamned leggings on. If she were anyone else I'd think she was doing it on purpose, forcing me to spend the day averting my eyes from the perfect curve of her ass, but I don't think Chloe has a clue. Today's pair is solid navy, and they cling to every inch of her from waist to ankle. She's wearing a long-sleeved white t-shirt that ends mid-hip, which does nothing to cover my view. I find myself wondering if her jacket will be long enough to cover her ass or if I'm going to be spending the day fighting a hard-on.

I follow her into the apartment and realize it's just a room—a studio apartment. A small kitchen with older appliances sits in an alcove to the left. Her bed—looks like a full size—is straight ahead, placed along the long wall. The bedding is fluffy and white, the bed neatly made. There's a small gray two-seat sofa under the window facing the door and a dresser on the short wall across from the bed that also serves as a TV stand. A Tiffany blue-painted trunk is serving as a coffee table in the few feet of space between the small sofa and the bed. A small wood table with two chairs painted in the same color as the trunk sit in the corner to my left and completes the apartment.

"Lucky for you I'm just about ready," she says, disappearing into the bathroom through a door at the end of the tiny excuse for a kitchen.

"Take your time," I say magnanimously as I inspect an arrangement of frames hanging by the tiny table. It looks like an assortment of shit from a garage sale, to be honest, but I stop to inspect it anyway. There's a needlepoint of an owl that looks to be at least two decades old. An old ticket to Hershey Park layered on top of a picture of a what appears to be pre-teenager Everly with her arms wrapped around an equally young version of Chloe. And a love note, written in colored pencil to Miss Scott from some asshole named Mark. Based on the handwriting Mark is probably eight, so I'll let it go.

I walk towards the bed to take a look out her windows. Shit, that bed is small. It's Chloe-sized, at best. I stop at the coffee table and look over her reading materials, grabbing the book on top and flipping it open as she walks back into the room midway into slinging her hair into a ponytail. "Chloe, you cannot be serious," I say with a laugh as I flip through the pages. "No one your age is using this," I say, holding up her copy of *Dating for Dummies*.

Her eyes widen and she stops midway through pulling her hair back. "That's a gift," she says, looking away. "For someone else. I was just about to wrap them up."

"Nice try, but you highlighted this copy, you little nerd," I say, closing the book with a shake of my head. I'm about to set it back on the coffee table when I see the second book and it hits me that she said she was about to wrap 'them' up. "*Sex for Dummies?*" Oh, fuck me, if she highlighted this one I will lose my shit.

I lock eyes with her and raise my brows in challenge as I grab it off the coffee table. Chloe shrieks and makes a dash towards me, diving for the book, but I've already got it. I raise my arm, holding it out of her reach as she collides with me, her tits pressing against my chest as she stretches her arm out, fingers extended, trying to make a grab for it. The top of her head only reaches my chin, so she doesn't have a shot at getting this book out of my hand. I should give it to her. I should. I will. In a minute. I hold it up, still closed, and look at the cover again while she makes a futile jump and her tits slide against my chest. She smells like fucking vanilla, God help me.

"Dr. Ruth K. Wertheimer," I read off the cover. "Chloe, come on. You are not getting sex tips from"—I glance at the cover again—"'America's favorite sex therapist.' She must be eighty years old."

"Well, I'm sure they had sex the same way in her day," she replies smartly, making another jump for the book. "And I'm a good student. I'm better with books than people."

"I can teach you anything you want to know," I hear myself saying. Jesus, that was creepy. She must think so too because she stops jumping and gives me an odd look. Then she steps onto the couch and yanks the book out of my hand.

"Very funny," she finally says, stepping off the couch and setting the book on the coffee table. "I know it's stupid, okay?" She stacks the two books together, squaring them up before she moves away from both me and the table, stopping to pick up the hair band that fell on the floor and sliding it over her wrist like a bracelet. "You don't have to tease me. I already know how ridiculous I am."

Fuck.

I need to remember to be careful with this girl. She's so... unsure of herself. She seems self-reliant, yet there's this undercurrent of doubt that I don't yet understand.

She walks across the studio and pulls a denim jacket from a small closet and shrugs into it, then picks up her bag and slings it over her shoulder. "Are you ready?"

I nod and follow her out, watching as she locks the door then tugs on it to make sure it's locked. We take the elevator down in silence then hit the sidewalk outside before she asks if we're walking or driving.

"Driving," I tell her, nodding to the parking spot I got in front of her building. I unlock the car and open the passenger door for her before walking around and getting behind the wheel.

"This is nice," she says, glancing around the interior of my Range Rover. "This is more James Bond than FBI though," she says, with a little wrinkle of her nose, her forehead creasing in concern.

"Are you disappointed?"

She shrugs. "It is a nice car," she says as she buckles herself in and crosses her legs, resting her hands on her knees. "But I don't think it's government-issued."

I laugh. "It's not. Does that disappoint you?" I ask, starting the car and merging into traffic.

"I guess it's okay." Another shrug.

I take a right onto the Schuylkill and ask if she's learned any new knock-knock jokes since I last saw her.

She turns her head and gives me a look. "Funny."

"I'm genuinely curious," I say. "You were killing it the other night."

"No. But speaking of killing, did you know that at any given time, there are between twenty and fifty serial killers in the United States? Did you know that?" She turns in her seat to look at me, her eyes wide with interest.

"That's quite the transition, from knock-knock jokes to serial killers," I comment while turning on the ramp to the I-676.

"Oh, yeah. Sorry." She shakes her head. "I just thought it would be fewer."

"Uh-huh."

"Like ten. I thought it would be ten. Maybe fifteen."

"One would think." I nod. Not really. Who thinks about this shit?

"What department do you work in anyway?"

"I'm almost sorry to tell you that it's not the BAU."

"That's probably a hard department to get into." She says it reassuringly and with a small nod and I fight not to laugh.

"Cyber crimes," I answer.

"Also very important," she says.

"Right," I agree, with a small nod. I imagine she's thinking I investigate credit-card fraud or piracy. She's cute.

"So do you have a gun?" she asks, and glances over at me like I might have one strapped to me that she didn't notice.

"Not on me, but yes. And it's government-issued," I add. "Does that make up for the car?"

"It does a little. Wait, where are we going?" she asks, throwing her hands up and glancing out the window at the expressway flying by.

"Dress shopping," I answer, already knowing the vague response will buy me all of five seconds.

"Why are we on the highway? Ohh, are we going to the outlet mall?" Her face lights up.

"New York," I answer.

"New York! That's a two-hour car ride!" I can see her looking at me from the corner of my eye like I'm an idiot and her voice is a little panicky. "Each way, Boyd. Two hours each way. This is going to take all day," she adds, stressing the word *all*. "Are there no stores in Philadelphia that meet your approval?"

"Did you have somewhere else you needed to be?" I ask, deflecting the question.

"Yes," she says. But it's lacking truth and comes out a little sullenly.

"Where? Is there a murder marathon on TV this afternoon, safety girl?"

"No!" she says. But she says it too quickly and fidgets in her seat.

"Holy shit, there is, isn't there? You're so weird." She's amazing.

"It's a *Criminal Minds* marathon, jerk," she retorts and this conversation starts to make sense. I'm competing with a fucking television show.

"So you wanted to get home to watch reruns, is what you're telling me?"

"Fine," she huffs. "I guess I can watch reruns another time."

"Thanks," I say drily. "That's big of you."

"You're welcome," she replies and I'm honestly not sure if she's being snarky or serious.

"Who's your favorite?" I ask. "On the show." Clearly I'm still stewing about competing with actors. It's probably the muscle guy, Agent Morgan. Which is fine, because she hasn't seen me naked yet. I can kick in a door when necessary too. Real ones, not stunt ones.

"Dr. Reid," she responds and I swear to fuck her voice is a little breathy when she says it.

"The nerd?"

"He's a genius, Boyd. And he's so cute." She's smiling.

"Fictional, Chloe. Fictional genius. No one has an IQ that high in real life." Fine. I've seen a few episodes. At least that fictional fucker never gets the girl.

"Hey, can I see your badge?"

Yeah, definite agent kink, I think as I reach into my back pocket and pull out my wallet and toss it to her. She flips it open and, seeing my official ID there as well, holds it close to inspect it, running her finger around the edge of the wallet as she does. She makes a little noise of approval as she flips it shut and hands it back to me.

"So can I ask you a question?" She wraps a strand of hair around her finger and examines the end of it before dropping it to look at me.

"Sure." I pass a slow-moving BMW and get comfortable, glancing at her to continue.

"Does the FBI monitor Google searches? Like, um, randomly? For normal people?"

"Normal people?"

"Non-criminal people."

"What kind of a question is that?"

"It's a real question!"

"But why are you asking it?"

"Because I Google some weird shit," she says, blowing out a breath and shaking her head. "I keep expecting someone to show up on my doorstep and ask what the heck I'm doing, but I'm just a really curious person and all the answers are right there, you know? Just click, click and there's your answer."

"I think you'll be okay," I assure her.

She nods and kicks off her sneakers and folds her legs up onto the seat, wrapping her arms around her bent knees and angling herself in my direction. "What are we going to talk about all day?"

She asks it casually, but her posture, while comfortable, is protective and the question itself tells me she's not the most comfortable in social situations.

"Am I making you nervous?"

"Not specifically. I'm just socially awkward with grown-ups. Total rock star with the under-tens, but grown-ups, not so much."

"Hence the knock-knock jokes."

"Right."

"We can talk about your FBI fetish," I offer, imagining Chloe in some naked roleplaying good times and wondering how long it's going to take to make that happen.

"I do not have a fetish!" she exclaims then pauses and after a beat, "What did Everly tell you?"

"Nothing," I say, laughing and trying for the first time in my life to actively remember words that came out of Everly's mouth. Every time I've seen that girl something inappropriate comes out of her mouth. I usually tune her crazy ass out. "Everly was your college roommate?"

"And my best friend growing up. I've known her forever."

"That must have been interesting," I say, a slight bit sarcastically.

She laughs. "I know she comes off a little crazy, but Everly's a great friend. The best."

"She seems like the kind of friend who would have gotten you grounded."

"No." Chloe laughs, but it's more of a giggle and I

wonder what she's thinking about.

"No sneaking out of the house?" I press. "Underage drinking? Sneaking around with boys?"

"Maybe a little," she admits. "But honestly, I'd probably have done nothing but read and study without her, so she was kind of a good bad influence."

"If you say so."

"Your sister likes her too!" she protests.

"Don't remind me."

"What about you?" she asks, reaching into her purse and pulling out her strawberry Chapstick. She uncaps it and runs it across her lips and I immediately think about her strawberry-coated lips wrapped around my dick. "Did you get grounded a lot?"

"What?"

"Did you get grounded a lot? When you were a kid?" she repeats, so I tear myself away from my fantasies about her lips on my dick and focus.

"Not really, no. I went to a boarding school from ninth grade on so I wasn't home. We got gated sometimes"—I glance over at her—"which was our version of detention, I suppose."

"Seriously?" Her eyes widen in surprise. "Your parents sent you away to boarding school?"

"No, they didn't send me. I asked to go."

"Why?"

"You know my dad was a senator," I say, glancing at her. "There was always some bullshit political fundraiser or rally they wanted me to attend. I hated it. Boarding school was an effective way for my parents to save face about why I wasn't around smiling and shaking hands."

"Oh." She's quiet. "That's kinda sad though."

I glance in her direction then back at the road. Is it? "I was happier at boarding school. Parenting didn't come naturally to my parents. I think it was a relief for all of us when I left."

She nods, interested.

"Plus my school was a lot closer to my grandparents in New Hampshire so I spent some weekends and breaks with them." Which I preferred.

She nods again, quiet for a moment.

"So how am I doing?" She asks, and I'm not sure what she's referring to.

"What do you mean?"

"Practicing. That's what we're doing, right? Practicing my conversational skills so I don't embarrass you in front of your friends and family next weekend?"

Oh, right.

"I believe in you. You're the one who needs to believe in yourself," I tell her.

"Okay," she says softly.

"Besides, you can't embarrass me."

"I can't?"

"Not possible."

I see her looking at me, thinking about that.

"Are you close with your parents?" I ask her, wanting to move the conversation back to something she's not going to overthink.

"No." She's shaking her head. "Not really, no. They got divorced when I was young. My dad moved to New York and I didn't see much of him after that." She glances at me then back out the window. "Apparently this two-hour drive was too far because he cancelled on me a lot. Meanwhile my mom kept herself pretty busy looking for a replacement for him. I think I was just in the way, you know?" She doesn't wait for an answer. "She was always dating some guy or another and then sobbing when they broke up. I felt bad, but I couldn't really deal with her."

"Because you were a child, Chloe, it wasn't your job to deal with her."

"I guess." She unfolds her legs and sets her feet on the floor, then crosses one leg over the other. "But I had Everly, so it was fine. She always included me. I even went on a few vacations with her family."

I guess Everly isn't a total menace, though it pains me to even mentally admit it.

"And even though she comes across a little strong," Chloe continues, "Everly was a good kid. We really didn't get into much trouble. She was the outgoing one though for sure. She kinda dragged me along on her adventures, but like I said, it was good for me or I'd have stayed in my comfort zone forever, you know?"

"Sure. Sometimes you need a little push."

"Exactly. Like I'd probably still be a virgin if it wasn't for Everly."

"You had a threesome with Everly?"

"What? Oh, my God, no!" She's flustered. "No! I meant—you know what I meant."

I do know. I flash her a grin. "But you've had sex?"

"I've had sex!" she protests. "I've totally had it. I have." She pulls one knee up to the seat and tucks it against her chest before crossing her arms around her bent knee and glancing back at me.

"Okay," I respond, cautious.

"It was okay or whatever."

Okay or whatever. Okay or whatever? I tap my index finger against the steering wheel for a second, unsure how to proceed on that without making her clam up.

"So what's with the *Sex for Dummies* book? It's been a while? It's like riding a bike, Chloe. It comes back to you. Just get back on the horse, so to speak." Jesus fuck. *Shut up, you idiot.*

She gnaws at her lower lip for a few seconds before responding. "I guess."

I flash a grin at her. "Or are you needing basic instructions?"

"I have the basics, thank you." I don't think she's going to say anything more, but then she continues. "Everly keeps telling me I just need someone who knows what they're doing, but I think it's me. You know? So I thought studying might help. I tried watching porn, but like..." She trails off.

"Like what?" I ask, while my dick tells me to shut the fuck up. He wants to focus on the image of Chloe watching porn.

"Like those people already like each other," she says, drumming her fingers against her bent knee. "Really like each other, right? They skip past all the weird stuff."

"What's the weird stuff?"

"For starters, do I ask him to come inside?"

I glance over at her, brow raised.

She slaps a hand over her eyes. "My house!" she clarifies. "Do I ask him to come inside my house? Or do I wait for him to bring it up? How close do I sit next to him? How obvious am I supposed to make it that I like him? Do I invite him to spend the night? Wait for him to make a move? Like, how do you know you're both on the same page? Maybe one of you is thinking you're about to have hot amazing sex and the other one of you is thinking about nachos." She sighs. "The dating transition from college to adulthood isn't easy. And I wasn't great at it in college. I get anxious in social settings."

"Chloe, promise me you won't repeat what I'm about to tell you."

"Okay."

"Ever. This is serious."

"Okay! I promise!" She tilts her head, a small smile on her face, amused with my dramatics.

"This is hard for me to say. And I hope I never have to say it again, but... Everly is right."

Chloe throws back her head and laughs and that's worth having to agree with Everly about something.

Nine

Chloe

Boyd's cocky. And hot. And kinda nice, even though he's cocky. I'd be a nervous wreck around him if I'd met him on a dating site. Not that we're dating. I almost laugh at the idea. Definitely not a date, he doesn't even have confidence that I can dress myself for our fake date. Whatever. But this car ride has been nice. Not as awkward as I thought it would be, and we're making great time; it's only taken us ninety minutes to reach the Lincoln Tunnel. I wonder, if Boyd got pulled over for speeding, would he flash his badge and get out of it?

As we enter the tunnel and the car is submerged in darkness I wonder what the heck he's going to pick out for me to wear. *It better not be too short,* I think, giving him a quick glance. I bet he's used to women in short sexy numbers. Maybe I can fake sexy for a night? Wait, this reminds me...

"Am I supposed to pretend it's a real date next weekend? Or am I supposed to pretend I'm there as your friend?"

The tunnel whizzes past as he drives and even though the tunnel is lit, it's much darker in the car than it was a few moments ago. He looks over at me, his face shadowed by the darkness, but I don't miss the analytical look on his face.

"Are you anxious about a fake date?"

"No!" Maybe just a little. "I'm just, you know, clarifying, because you never said."

"It's a real fake date," he says, looking a little annoyed.

"Real fake," I repeat. "That is super confusing."

"Just pretend you like me."

"I don't dislike you," I offer helpfully. "You're okay."

He runs his tongue along his bottom lip and glances at me out of the side of his eye.

"What? I'm just agreeing that it won't be horribly hard to pretend to like you." He's sort of confusing, this guy.

"Great," he says as he slows the car as we exit the tunnel and roll up to a traffic light.

"Look, I'm sure you're not used to women faking it with you, but this fake date was your idea, not mine."

"You're right. I'm not used to women faking it with me." He smirks. He's not even looking at me, his attention on the road ahead of him, so I think he's smirking to himself. Asshole.

Yet.

Yet I can't help but think he's earned that smirk. I can admit I'm curious. Even if it's never going to happen, my imagination is not nearly as socially awkward as I am. So I can visualize him on top of me. Holding himself above me with those arms—he has really nice arms. He's wearing a navy sweater and he's pushed the sleeves up to the elbow at some point during this drive so I've had time to observe them close up, and, yeah. Arm porn. I bet he has no problems unscrewing those tough lids on jars. Or fucking. Either or.

"Is it our first date? This wedding? Or have we been seeing each other a while?"

He nods his head slowly, like he approves of my

planning our fake dating history. "Not a first date, but it's a new relationship. How's that?"

"Okay, I can do that."

I'm quiet while Boyd navigates the streets of Manhattan. He seems intent on a destination and while I'm curious, I'm happy to go along with the flow. It's sorta nice having someone take charge of the day. New York has this energy about it, it's fun to watch it from the comfort of the car. Philadelphia's a huge city too, but nothing like the chaos of Manhattan. Philly is more my speed on a day-to-day basis, but New York for a day will be fun.

Boyd turns down 17th and pulls into a garage. I slide my feet back into my sneakers and apply a fresh layer of Chapstick while Boyd finds a parking spot. I didn't catch the cross street when we pulled in, but we exit the garage and end up on 5th Avenue after a short block with Boyd guiding our direction.

"We have to make a stop first," he says, sliding a pair of sunglasses over his eyes, his demeanor serious.

"Okay," I agree, shrugging. We walk a couple of blocks to 19th then head west. We don't talk, but the silence isn't weird. If you can even call it silence. New York is loud and it seems we're both content to listen to the background sounds of people yelling, horns blaring and tires screeching.

We walk half a block before Boyd stops, holding a door open for me to enter. His eyes are hidden behind the sunglasses but the smile on his face tells me he's amused. I stop and look up. Dough. I glance past him into the store. It's a donut shop called Dough, how cute is that? "You brought me to a donut shop?"

"You don't like donuts?" The tone of his question is fake incredulous. "Are you sure? I really thought I nailed this after seeing those pants of yours."

I roll my eyes in his face as he laughs. "You're an ass." But I enter the shop all the same because really, who doesn't love donuts? And holy cow, the smells wafting from the door are calling to me. We make our way to the end of the line and I bounce on my toes to read the menu board over people's heads. Ohh... specialty donuts. How will I choose? We reach the front and Boyd indicates I should order first. I select a Nutella donut. And a dulce de leche. And a pumpkin. It's seasonal, I can't pass that up. Plus who knows when I'll be back here again?

"I'm sorry, were you ordering for both of us?" Boyd deadpans.

"Shut up."

He orders a cinnamon sugar donut then asks if I want a coffee too. Is he crazy? One donut? "He wants a salted chocolate caramel donut too," I tell the girl taking our order. "And we'll take two coffees."

I grab both coffees and walk over to the coffee station, Boyd behind me with the donuts.

"There is no way you're eating four donuts." He shakes his head at me, a smile on his lips.

"No," I agree. "But I can *taste* four donuts."

He nods. "That was a nice girlfriend move back there."

"What?" I ask, confused by what he means. I remove the lid from my coffee and add in a couple of fake sugars and creamer. "Do you want anything added to yours?" I nod towards the second cup.

"Black is fine," he says. "The 'ordering food for me so you can eat it' thing." He gestures to the counter. "You're already a professional."

"Thanks."

"Although I've never had a date order three donuts

for themselves to start with." He winks.

"Like you take dates out for donuts," I retort sarcastically.

"No? Where do I take them?" he asks, guiding me to a couple of empty stools at the window counter looking out over 19th Street. I set the coffees down and hop up on the stool, my feet resting on the metal stool rung. Boyd sprawls on his stool, one foot flat on the floor, the other knee bent, his body turned towards mine. I give him a quick once-over before answering. I can't help it.

"The gym. I think you take them to the gym. Or ask them out at the gym and then take them for drinks and sex."

He looks like he's thinking about that as he opens the donut box between us and picks up the cinnamon sugar. "Am I allowed to eat this one?" he asks, brows raised.

"Of course, silly, that one's yours." I wonder what it tastes like though, giving it another glance as I pick up the dulce de leche and take a bite before setting it back in the box. I take a sip of coffee before moving on to the pumpkin, while eyeing the salted chocolate caramel and the Nutella. I think I'll try the salted chocolate caramel before the Nutella. Yup, that's my game plan. I put down the pumpkin and pick up the next donut and catch Boyd looking at me.

"What?"

"Nothing." He shakes his head, watching me stuff the salted chocolate into my mouth.

"You should try the pumpkin," I offer while eyeing the cinnamon sugar in his hand again. "It's seasonal," I add, as a sales pitch.

He hands me his half-eaten cinnamon sugar and I grin before taking a bite and handing the rest back. "Thanks," I tell him after another sip of coffee. "That was a good palate cleanser before the main event."

"A donut palate cleanser?"

"Yup." He finishes off his donut while I pick up the Nutella. "Do you want a bite of this one? Because I may not be able to stop once I start."

He looks from me to the donut then out the front window before declining, a distracted look on his face. He's probably in a hurry to get shopping.

I take a bite, careful not to dump the powdered sugar topping all over my shirt. Luckily I'm wearing white though, so it'd blend in anyway. The Nutella hits my tongue and I moan. Perfection. I might have to finish this entire donut. I take another bite and wiggle in my seat in sugar bliss while Boyd laughs at me. He picks up the pumpkin and polishes it off as I take another bite of Nutella nirvana. When I'm done I wipe my hands off with a paper napkin and grab my cup. Boyd's staring at me like he's ready to go.

"You've got powdered sugar," he says and reaches over, using his thumb to wipe the corner of my mouth. I freeze, surprised that he's touching me and feeling like it's oddly intimate for him to be wiping my lip for me, yet liking it. I like it a lot, but this is Boyd, so I don't think it means anything—even though my heart is racing and his eyes are magnetic. Then he's tucking a strand of hair behind my ear and standing and the moment is over.

"Let's go," he says, pulling his sunglasses off the collar of his shirt and sliding them on.

Okay, sure. Let's go. Whatever just happened was totally in my mind obviously. We exit Dough, heading the opposite direction on 19th Street.

"Oh, a Container Store," I gush upon seeing the organizational store.

"Does that get you all hot and bothered, Chloe? Did

you want to stop?"

"Shut up," I say as we cross the street. "Maybe later." We turn on 6th Avenue then on 17th and a short walk later we're outside of Barney's. I stop outside the doors. "Seriously?"

"What's wrong with Barney's?" he asks.

"It seems a little stuffy."

"The wedding will be a little stuffy too," he says, removing his sunglasses and sliding them over his shirt collar. "Remember we're practicing," he adds and then grabs my hand and walks me inside.

Why the heck is he holding my hand? He doesn't let go of it though, instead he keeps walking with my hand in his like we're a couple. I start to panic before I remember we're practicing. *Deep breath, go with the flow, Chloe.* By the time we reach the women's dress department I'm enjoying the hand-holding. But then I start to wonder if my hand is sweating and I freak out again. At that point we're intercepted by a saleswoman offering her assistance and Boyd drops my hand.

And then drapes his arm over my shoulder.

I honestly don't even hear the exchange between them because all I can focus on is the feel of Boyd's arm wrapped around me. And the way his chest feels where our bodies connect. It feels hard. Really freaking solid. And he smells good. I don't have any other coherent thoughts beyond that. And I think I missed a bunch while I was zoning out about Boyd's chest because the next thing I know I'm inside of a fitting room filled with dresses.

Except one isn't a dress. It's a sparkly romper. Short with a plunging neckline. Huh. I slip into it out of sheer curiosity and almost laugh at my reflection. No way. The shorts on this thing are shorter than the pajama bottoms

I sleep in. I think these are sequin-covered pajamas.

I open the fitting room door and step out, expecting Boyd to laugh with me over the ridiculousness of this outfit, but when he glances up from his phone he stills and then his eyes seem to move in slow motion from my head to my toes. And he doesn't appear to find this outfit as amusing as I do. "Take that off."

"I didn't pick it out!" I protest, still thinking it's kinda funny.

"You're not wearing that in public."

Okay, wow. No, I wasn't going to wear this past the dressing room, but I didn't think it looked that bad on me; he didn't have to be a jerk about it. As I turn away he mutters, "Jesus, that barely covers your ass," and then he's calling out for Angie, the saleswoman, as I shut the fitting room door and examine myself in the mirror. It's not anything I would wear, but it's kinda hot.

I try on several more, discarding them for one reason or another; a couple are placed on the maybe pile, until I slip into the one I'm wearing now. It's black lace over a nude lining. Long sleeves and the neckline rests on my collarbone, but the hemline ends a few inches above my knees. It's my kind of sexy, I think. It's more classy than risqué. The nude lining covers everything, of course, but makes the dress pop more than a black lining would have. I knot my hair on top of my head to get a visual of the final look and stand on my tiptoes to check out what it would look like with heels. I'm in love with this dress.

"Let's see it," Boyd calls from outside the dressing room.

"How do you know I like this one enough to come out?"

"Because you've been in the same dress for five minutes and you're wearing pretend heels," he answers drily.

Wait. I fling open the door. "Are you watching me under the fitting room door? That's kind of pervy."

He smiles slowly. "All I can see are your feet to mid calf."

"Maybe you have a foot fetish."

He glances down at my bare feet and then stands, moving closer until he's inches away. I look up at him and my breath catches. Holy shit, is he going to kiss me? I stop breathing as he places his hands on my shoulders and then he turns me, and I breathe again as his fingers move to the zipper. Right, I forgot I was only half zipped. I couldn't reach far enough to zip it to the top. I try not to fidget as he zips me, but I wish he would zip a little faster.

"Perfect," he murmurs once the zipper reaches the top.

"The dress is perfect?" I question, turning around again and holding my arms out from my body, examining the sleeves.

He meets my eyes and a second passes before he confirms. "Yes, the dress is perfect."

I change back into my own clothes while Boyd pays for the dress, Angie retrieving it from the fitting room and zipping it into a dress bag with a Barney's New York logo on the outside. On our way to shoes we pass the women's lingerie department. Or at least I pass women's lingerie. Boyd stops. It takes me a few steps for me to notice and when I turn around he angles his head towards the department, his face serious.

"No," I respond as I turn back around and keep walking. I can hear him laughing as he catches up with me.

"Are you sure? I'm buying."

"Firm no, Boyd. I have underwear, thank you. The shopping trip is weird enough."

"Why is it weird?" He looks genuinely puzzled.

"I don't know, it feels weird that you're buying me things."

"Don't worry about it," he says, picking up a heel he can't possibly expect me to wear. "I have plenty of money. I didn't even earn it. Hell, my parents didn't even earn it."

I stop with a shoe in my hand and stare at him wide-eyed. "Did you steal it?"

"What? No." He laughs, looking genuinely amused. "I... are you serious?"

Um, am I? "Well, no, you probably wouldn't have passed the FBI background check if you came from a family of gypsies." Oh, wait, I remember now. Sophie came into some kind of an inheritance when Boyd found her last year. She's his half-sister, a child his father had from an affair that no one knew about. She didn't even know the deceased senator was her dad or that she had a sibling until Boyd found her. "You have an inheritance?"

He nods.

"So why do you work?"

"Why wouldn't I work?" He looks genuinely confused. "My grandpa would have kicked my ass if I hadn't taken school seriously and selected my own career path. Besides, I like what I do."

"What was the family career path? Your dad was a politician, so I assume he wasn't in the family business."

"Candy."

"You're joking."

"Nope." He shakes his head, laughing. "I thought you knew."

"Sophie never mentioned it." I slide on one pair of the

heels the saleswoman—Catie this time—has brought out and stand, walking a few steps in the shoe department to get a feel for them.

"Try these," Boyd instructs, handing me the higher pair. I take a seat and switch them out then stand again. These aren't heels, they're stilettos. "We'll take those," Boyd says, handing his card to Catie while I'm still practice-walking in them.

"Boyd, I don't know," I murmur. But I'm not sure they're me. "These are"—I drop my voice—"fuck-me heels."

"I don't see how that's a problem," he says, dragging his eyes up to my face. "You're practicing, remember?"

"They look okay?" I'm sort of in love with them already. Not that I'll have anywhere to wear them besides this wedding. I don't think they go with my leggings, that's for sure. The dress is fairly modest though, the heels will sex it up a little but not too much.

"They look fantastic," Boyd answers. "Are they comfortable?"

"They are. But do you think they're safe? What if I trip in them?"

"I'll catch you," he quips.

It's not like I'm going to jog in them, I think with a shrug. I take them off and Boyd hands them over to the saleswoman to box up while I put my sneakers back on. "Thanks for the shoes, sugar," I say and add a dramatic wink.

TEN
BOYD

I'm not sure I've ever gone to this much effort to spend time with a girl before, but as we exit the store I'm not ready for the day to be over. We walk back in the direction of the car, Chloe swinging the bag with her shoes and me carrying the dress bag slung over my shoulder. She doesn't see this as a date so she's relaxed and I want to hold onto that a little bit longer. We walk in comfortable silence down 17th and when we should cut down 6th to grab the car on 18th I keep walking.

"Isn't the car down that way?" Chloe asks, starting to recognize that we're back at the same intersection we walked past earlier on the way to Dough.

"I need to grab something from American Apparel," I tell her, remembering we passed one on earlier today on the way to Dough.

"Sure." She shrugs. "No problem." I like her like this, when she's not on guard. Although she's pretty damn funny when she's nervous too.

I drag her into American Apparel and grab some crewneck t-shirts I don't really need while Chloe pauses in front of a display of raglan tees. So I get a couple of those too.

"So what made you go into law enforcement instead of the candy business?" she asks when we're back outside.

"Women," I tell her and lead her down 19th towards Broadway, for no other reason than it's the opposite direction from the car. She gives me a signature Chloe dirty look and I laugh. "I'm kidding. I was never going into the candy business. I'm on the board because my grandfather asked me to be on it, but business has never been my interest. I've been into technology since I was a kid. It started with hacking game apps, making workarounds to beat the game. That sort of stuff. Let's just say it progressed from there. Then the FBI recruited me shortly after college."

"You must be pretty talented," she says innocently.

"You have no idea," I saw slowly, my eyes not leaving hers. She gets my meaning and her eyes widen and she gnaws on her lower lip.

"I'm sure," she agrees, clearly at a loss in how to reply. She slows in front of a window display at Fishs Eddy. "Let's go in here," she says. She bounces on her toes a little when she says it. I glance at the window display— looks like an assortment of shit from Grandma's garage sale, but if it puts a smile on her face, I'm in. I grab the door and follow her inside.

I trail her through the store watching her make a loop, pausing at things that interest her, running her fingers across items of particular interest. I have no idea what I've stumbled into. The store is jam-packed from front to back with the oddest assortment of housewares shit. But Chloe is enthralled. Much of it has a funky vintage flair and reminds me a bit of the assortment of picture frames she had hung in her apartment. After looking at everything she goes back through the store a second time and picks up a small selection of items, chattering about Christmas before heading to the register. It's October so

I'm not sure what the fuck she's talking about, but I don't say anything.

We exit the store and continue walking around the Flatiron district, ducking into stores that catch her interest. We end up in front of Beecher's.

"Let's have dinner." I nod to the shop. "They have a restaurant downstairs."

"You couldn't get a date for tonight either?" She stops dead on the sidewalk, eyebrow raised in disbelief.

"You need the practice. Come on," I tell her, holding the door open. She shakes her head and rolls her eyes but enters the store. It's early so we're seated immediately. Chloe buries her head in the menu and I start to wonder if I imagined the way she looked at me back at the donut shop when she snaps the menu closed and speaks.

"Why did the orange go out with the prune?"

I can feel my lips pull into a smile as much as I attempt to resist and keep a straight face. "You're nervous? We're just practicing, remember?"

She twists in her seat a little and nods. "True."

The waitress stops by and takes our orders. Steak for me, macaroni and cheese for Chloe.

"Macaroni and cheese?" I ask, my tone teasing and brow lifted.

"We're in a restaurant underneath a cheese shop, Boyd," she says, stressing the word cheese. "I bet it's the best macaroni and cheese in the world and you're gonna be so jealous when it gets here."

"If you say so."

"You will be."

"So why did the orange go out with the prune anyway?"

She blinks for a second then smiles. "Because he couldn't find a date!" Then she laughs. "Get it? Date?

Like the fruit?"

"Got it." I incline my head in acknowledgment. "Speaking of dates, do you have any this week? Anything I can prep you for?" How the fuck am I supposed to deal with her dating? What if she finds some guy who likes these ridiculous second-grade jokes and she wants to fuck him? That's not going to work for me.

"No." She shakes her head, rolling her eyes at herself. "Last week was an anomaly to be honest. I don't get out that much." I wait for her to laugh or crack a smile, but she picks up a piece of bread and rips off a tiny chunk instead. "There was this one guy I've been talking to for weeks online."

Well, that's fucking great.

"But then he asked me to get a tattoo. Which is weird, right?" She looks to me for confirmation but keeps speaking without giving me a chance to reply. "I never even met him. But he asked me to get a tattoo. Of his name. On my freaking body."

Fuck, no.

"He said to put it on my hip or somewhere sexy." She leans in closer and lowers her voice. "He said this way he would know that I'm not sleeping with anyone else."

I eye her for a moment. "You're making that up."

"I'm not." She shakes her head back and forth. "That is a true story." She punctuates her sentence with a fingertip in the air. "Anyway, I should spend some time studying those books before I go on another date." She's serious.

"Chloe," I groan. "Throw those ridiculous books away. You need real-life practice, not a book."

She pauses, having just stuffed the piece of bread into her mouth, and stares at me. I can practically hear her mind whirring, wondering if I'm referring to real-life sex practice or real-life dating practice. I'm definitely referring to sex.

"Um, yeah," she mumbles noncommittally and continues chewing.

The waitress arrives with our orders and Chloe digs in, emitting a happy little sigh as a cheesy noodle hits her tongue. She takes another bite and moans. She wiggles in her chair but I don't think it's for the same reason that I've just had to adjust my goddamned cock.

"See! You're jealous, aren't you?" she asks, eyes wide when she notices me staring at her. I don't think gluttony is the correct deadly sin that I'm feeling, but I attempt to look chagrined as I wave my fork at her plate.

"You might have out-ordered me with the macaroni and cheese, Chloe."

She tilts her head slightly to the side and offers me a funny half smile before she nods and pushes her plate towards me. "It's okay, we can share."

Later when the bill arrives Chloe digs out her wallet.

"I've got it," I tell her. Why the fuck is she trying to pay?

"But it's not a date. Why should you pay?"

"I've got it," I repeat. "You can owe me another favor," I add when she looks like she's going to object again. "If that makes you feel better."

She wrinkles her nose at me. "I feel like you're stacking up all the favors. How do I get a favor?"

"Would you like a favor?" Please let it be dirty.

She thinks about it and shrugs.

On the drive home she tells me about her class. About the kids, the school, her classroom, her upcoming lesson plans. We talk a little bit more about what it was like for me to grow up as the son of a US Senator. I find myself talking to her about the shock of finding out about

Sophie—finding out that I had a half-sister who was obviously born while our father was married to my mother. About realizing that my mother knew about Sophie's existence all along. I tell her that looking back from an adult perspective I've realized how much the tension between my parents contributed to me choosing boarding school. Because while they'd always put on a happy facade—both in public and at home—there was always something that felt off.

When we arrive at her apartment I find a place to park on the street before she has a chance to question it and grab her bags from the back of the car. She could easily carry these items herself, so I keep her talking and walk her inside. When we reach her unit she looks at the bags in my hands and frowns before turning to unlock the door.

"I could have carried that myself. You didn't need to park."

I walk inside of her apartment and place the bags on her tiny kitchen table, laying the garment bag over one of the chairs. When I turn she's still at the door two feet away removing her key from the lock. I have her pressed against the open door and my lips on hers before she even looks up. She freezes. Four long seconds. Maybe five. My fingers are behind her neck, my thumb on her cheek angling her mouth where I want it. And during those several seconds I berate myself for pushing her. Then I softly bite her bottom lip and she starts to breathe again, a tiny sigh that seems to move through her entire body because she relaxes and kisses me back. I move closer, closing the inch-wide gap between our bodies, the soft curves of her breasts pressing into my chest as I move my other hand to her hair.

When I finally break the kiss and step back, she blinks,

eyes dazed. Her bewilderment is quickly replaced with confusion and then a flicker of apprehension flashes through her eyes. I've pushed this too soon.

"Well, I'm gonna go," she says, jingling the keys in her hand.

"We're in your apartment," I point out, trying not to laugh.

"Oh, yeah," she agrees, glancing around.

"That's what I'd have done if this was a date," I say, giving her an out. I keep my eyes on hers and rub my thumb across my bottom lip, remembering the feel of her mouth on mine. "And it wasn't weird, right? You're worried about nothing." The creases around her eyes ease and she relaxes.

"Right." She nods. "Well, you're good at it," she adds with a shake of her head and a laugh.

"I'll call you with the details for next weekend," I tell her. And then I get the hell out.

Eleven

Chloe

Boyd Gallagher can kiss. I've thought about his lips—that kiss—a few times more than I care to admit. A few dozen more times. He shocked me, caught me off guard. I wasn't anticipating it, that's for sure.

So I froze, unsure of what was happening. Unsure of how I felt about it. Then he pressed closer, kissing me deeper, and I stopped caring about what was happening. I stopped thinking about it and just enjoyed it—whatever 'it' was. And holy shit, Boyd Gallagher can make you forget. His lips can drive every single thought out of your head.

Well, maybe not every thought, because I managed to have a whole slew of inappropriate ones while his lips were pressed to mine. Thoughts about how no man has ever kissed me quite like that before. Thoughts of how my nipples felt pressed against his chest, how hard and warm he felt even through the layers of clothing separating us. I thought about how the skin on the back of my neck tingled where his fingers were wrapped, pulling me to him. I thought about how good it all felt without being too much. That while he ambushed me with the kiss his hands remained on my neck and pressed against the door next to my head. And finally, I had thoughts about how turned on I was. Like ready to unbuckle his pants turned on.

And then he broke the kiss and took a step back.

After that all my insecurities returned in a heartbeat and I panicked. Why was he kissing me? What did it mean? Did he like it? Did he want to do it again? Or did he never want to kiss me again? How long did I freeze at the beginning? Does he think I'm weird? Does he like me? Do I like him? Most importantly, what if I like him and it doesn't work out?

What if we have sex and it's bad and he never talks to me again? Or what if we have sex and it's bad but he thinks it's good and wants to keep having terrible sex with me? What if we get together and it doesn't work out and then I have to explain it to my friends, which includes his sister?

So yes, I'll admit that I panicked. I'm not a hasty thinker; I need a moment to process things or I feel cornered and I freak out. I'm like that with everything—apartment leases, pizza toppings, kissing. I just need a minute to think.

But then he rubbed his bottom lip with his thumb and told me that's what he'd have done if we were on a real date. Because he's my dating tutor or something now. When exactly did that happen anyway? The details get fuzzy when I'm around Boyd. He arrested my date. I asked him not to say anything about it to Everly or his sister Sophie. And that spiraled into me owing him a favor and him providing me with dating advice. I think. He's sort of confusing.

I was a mass of mixed feelings after that kiss. Excited, terrified, confused, aroused. My heart was racing—hell, it still races a little when I think about it. I felt relief that it wasn't real because it let me off the hook from thinking about what that would mean. Yet I felt disappointed and foolish for the same reason. So I said nothing—I needed another minute to process this twist—and before I could decide if I wanted to slap him or drag him back for more, he walked out the door, tossing out something about calling me with the details for next weekend.

On Wednesday he texted.

Boyd: Friday night. 8pm.

Chloe: ???

Boyd: What's ??? Confusing?

Chloe: I thought you said the wedding was on Saturday?

Boyd: It is.

Chloe: Then why do I need to see you on Friday?

Boyd: You need the practice. We'll call it a date rehearsal.

Chloe: Are you serious right now?

Boyd: Dress comfortably. You can wear some of those godforsaken leggings you love. Wait, don't. Sweatpants would be better. Baggy sweatpants.

Chloe: WTF are you talking about?

Boyd: See you Friday.

Chloe: Um, no.

Boyd: No you don't own any sweatpants?

Chloe: No, I won't see you on Friday.

Boyd: You will.

Chloe: What do we need to rehearse? You picked out the dress and shoes yourself. AND you've already rehearsed kissing me. Do you need to practice kissing me again? That was rude by the way. R.U.D.E. And if you think this favor I owe you includes making out with you in front of your family you can think again.

Boyd: So as long as my family isn't watching it's okay? Deal.

Chloe: ....

Boyd: ....

The arrogant bastard shows up on Friday night at a quarter to eight. He's wearing jeans that fit him perfectly, a long-sleeved black Henley and a smug smile—which drops from his face as his eyes trail over my legging-clad legs.

"Fucking leggings," he mutters and walks inside my apartment without waiting for an invitation. I shut the door behind him and cross my arms across my chest while resting my weight on one hip, shooting Boyd with the most snarky expression I can manage.

"I'm busy, Boyd, what do you need?"

I mean seriously, what does he need? He cannot be

hard up for female companionship on a Friday evening and as lovely as it is that he's taken me on some sort of charity case, he's got to have better things to do.

"You seem pretty busy," he agrees, nodding towards my TV. I'm in the middle of a *Dateline* episode about a murder.

I sigh and roll my eyes, uncrossing my arms to wave a hand at him, indicating he should get to his point.

"I need you to pack," he says.

Pack for what? I get a sinking feeling in my stomach as it occurs to me that Boyd's never exactly said where this wedding is. Did I ever ask? Or did I just assume it was in the general Philadelphia area? I watch him as he strolls through my tiny studio apartment, his gaze roaming over my things while mine roams over him. Dammit, that shirt looks good on him. Freaking clingy cotton.

"What are you talking about?" I question when he doesn't elaborate further. "Pack for what?"

He turns from the window, running his hand along his jaw. "Oh." He pauses and drops his hand. "Did I forget to mention that the wedding is in Vail?"

"Vail!" I shriek. "Vail, Colorado? I can't go with you to Colorado! It's halfway across the country!"

"So?" He shakes his head, the skin around his eyes creasing in amusement. "Philadelphia, Vail. What's the difference? I still have to go to this wedding, I still need to bring a date and you still have a new dress to wear," he says, pointing to the dress still hanging in the store carrier bag, the hanger hooked over the top of my closet door. "Where's your suitcase?" he asks, walking over to the closet and opening the door.

"Hey!" I protest.

He ignores me and, spotting my rolling suitcase on the top shelf—the shelf I need to stand on top of a chair to reach—he makes an easy reach for it and pulls it down. And yes, I catch a glimpse of his rock-hard abs when his shirt rises. I don't stand a chance here, do I?

"I'm a teacher, Boyd. I can't just miss class to do you a favor."

He drops the suitcase on my bed and shoots me a smugly satisfied look. "What kind of amateur do you think I am? I know you're off on Monday for Columbus Day. I'll have you home by dinner time on Monday, Cinderella."

"I don't have a plane ticket," I say, waving my arms in exasperation. He makes everything sound so easy.

He unzips my suitcase and lays it open ready for me to fill. "You don't need a ticket. Any other objections?"

"This is way bigger than the favor I owe you. Huge," I add, holding my hands apart to indicate something big.

"Fine. So I owe you a favor. Feel free to make it sexual."

"You wish," I snap back. What am I, sixteen? Wait, did he just offer to have sex with me? Or is he teasing me? I don't really get it. I sigh loudly and dramatically. "What time is our flight?" I ask, opening a dresser drawer under my television. I stop and glance over at him when he doesn't respond. He raises one eyebrow and doesn't say anything. "Oh," I reply mockingly. "You have a private plane, don't you? We're taking your candy plane to Vail."

"It's not technically a candy plane, but I'll suggest having it covered in gumdrops at the next board meeting I show up for. Any other objections?"

"This seems like an inappropriate use of company resources for a company you're barely involved in and own a fraction of." I'm just stalling now. Clearly I'm going to Vail.

"We really need to work on your flattery skills," he deadpans as he moves closer, looking amused as he stops in front of me. "I pay a fee to use the jet. I can put you in touch with someone at the IRS if you want to verify everything is on the up and up." Then he glances into the drawer I've opened and his lip twitches. "Do you need help packing?"

It's my underwear drawer, because of course that's the one I've left hanging open.

"Go away." I stick my elbow in his ribs and force him to step back. "Sit on the couch and keep your hands to yourself," I instruct, then follow him to the sofa and grab my *Dating* and *Sex for Dummies* books off the coffee table and shove them into my sock drawer while he laughs. "You're making me miss my show," I gripe as I toss things into the suitcase.

"Your show? You sound like you're eighty." He glances at the TV behind me then back to me. "*Murder on Mason Lane*," he says. "It was the neighbor. She was committing Medicare fraud using the victim's deceased wife's information. He caught on so she killed him."

I gasp. "You spoiler! You spoiling spoiler who spoils!" Then I shrug. "This is a new episode. You don't even know that. It's the daughter. She killed him. I've had her pegged since the first commercial break."

"You're cute."

"Just you wait," I tell him, very satisfied with myself. I'm really good at guessing whodunnit.

"Sorry, you murder nerd, I worked on this case two years ago. It's the neighbor."

"Really?" I drop my makeup bag into the suitcase and check to see if he's teasing me.

"I swear. I'll tell you all the good shit the show left out once we're on the plane."

I survey Boyd with interest. I do have a lot of questions. "I thought you were in cyber crimes, not murder."

"Murder isn't a department," he replies, shaking his head at me.

"You know what I mean."

"Most crimes have a cyber component to them these days. There's always a cyber trail."

Shit, that's hot.

TWELVE
BOYD

I get her into the car and to the airport without any more complaining about this weekend trip. I knew springing it on her at the last moment was the way to go. Once she'd had a few moments to mull it over and argue with me she was fine. If I'd given her all week to think about it she'd have been a nervous wreck and talked herself out of it.

At least she's good until we reach the plane. She pauses on the steps and turns to look at me, wrinkling her nose in suspicion.

"There better not be a bed on this plane, creep."

I laugh and shake my head. "I don't think any of the planes have a bedroom."

"Planes? There's more than one? Dang, I should have taken Everly seriously that time she suggested we open a candy store back when we were eight." She jogs up the remaining steps—her leggings-covered ass directly in my line of sight—and I stifle a groan and try to focus on the pilot greeting us at the top of the stairs before I get a fucking hard-on like a teenager.

We take a couple of oversized seats next to each other and the lone flight attendant on the flight gives us blankets and dims the lights after verifying that we don't want anything. As soon as we're airborne I show Chloe how to recline the seat and kick up the footrest and she flashes me an awed grin that makes me pause. When is the last time I saw someone get excited about the equivalent of a La-Z-Boy? Have I ever? She's not the first girl I've taken on a private jet, but I'm positive she's the only girl who's ever scowled at me about it.

If I'd taken Vanessa this weekend we'd have been fucking in the bathroom the moment the plane leveled out. But I wasn't interested in bringing Vanessa. Or any of the other women I have listed in my phone who would have been happy to go. I was interested in dragging Chloe on this trip and I'm not even sure she likes me. She's attracted to me, yes, but does she like me?

Jesus, what the fuck is wrong with me? Why do I care if she likes me? Liking me enough to fuck me is all that I should care about. Yet I find myself strangely interested in this girl. She's beautiful. Awkward, sarcastic and captivating. Yet possibly the most skeptical girl I've ever met. There's something about her that makes me want to dig a little deeper with her. She's a challenge. Possibly a long-term challenge and I'll play this favor game with her—for her—if that's what it takes to keep her from running.

"Tell me!" She's turned on her side facing me, the blanket draped over her from shoulder to toes. Her eyes are wide and inquisitive. What does she want me to tell her? I review the last few minutes and try to remember what we've been talking about. I give up and raise an eyebrow in question.

"*Murder on Mason Lane!*" she replies while slapping her palm against the seat in a 'how could you forget' kind of way. Then she narrows her eyes skeptically. They're so fucking pretty, her eyes. They're green and she might have a coat of mascara on her lashes but nothing else. I'm sure she'd be stunning with all that shit girls put on their eyes, but she doesn't need it. She's naturally gorgeous, even when she's staring at me with cynicism. "Did you work on that case or were you lying to get me on this plane?"

Ahh, the stupid case featured on *Dateline* that I promised to tell her more about. I can't say a woman's ever had any interest in using me for an inside scoop before—in anything to do with my job other than the handcuffs. The handcuffs are pretty popular, if I'm being honest.

So I give her all the details from the Mason Lane case, the details too boring to make it into a one-hour television episode. I talk until her pretty eyes droop and close, fatigue finally winning out over her quest for answers. I watch her sleep and, yes, it occurs to me that it might be a bit creepy but I don't care. Her eyelashes rest against her perfect creamy skin. Her eyebrows are a delicate arch. Her hair—which I got a feel of last week when I kissed her—is lying across her cheek. It's soft and glossy and I want more than a brush of it against my hand. I want to wrap it around my fist while I move inside of her. Or thread my fingers through it while her lips are wrapped around my cock. I want it fanning over my chest after I've made her come and she's lying on top of me, relaxed and sated.

I reach over and brush it over her ear and she blinks at me, not really awake. She emits a small murmur and smiles, then closes her eyes again and nods off, her arm sliding from her seat to mine. I slip my hand in hers as I close my eyes and let sleep overtake me.

***

We touch down in the morning at the regional airport

just outside of Vail. We're outside the airport with our luggage in hand minutes after touching the ground. Flying private never gets old.

"Boyd! Holy wow. Have you seen this?" Chloe is spinning around, taking in the mountain views that hit you no matter which way you're facing.

"I have," I respond with a quick nod while opening the back of the SUV I arranged for our stay. I stow our bags in the back then slam the door closed and look at her. The Rocky Mountains surround us—the vista is stunning, no doubt. But it's her I can't take my eyes off of.

"You've been here before?" She stops gaping at the view to focus on me.

"I have." I guide her to the passenger side of the SUV and open the door for her. "We'll come back when there's snow," I say and she gives me an odd look, then stops short and squeals.

"You rented a Suburban!" she says, laughing.

"I thought it was the least I could do, since you're doing me this favor and all."

"True," she agrees and then grabs the interior roof handle and hikes herself into the passenger seat. I resist from wrapping my hands around her waist to help. Barely. "Maybe this will motivate you to work your way up and get your own government-issued Suburban," she jokes as she pulls the seatbelt across her body and snaps it into place.

"Cute." I close her door and cross to the driver's side. Within five minutes we're on Highway 6 headed east towards Vail.

"I can see now why you had to bring a fake date this weekend," Chloe mentions while rooting around in her bag and coming up with a pair of sunglasses that she slides on before tucking her knee up on the seat and turning towards me.

"Oh, yeah? Why is that?"

"The candy plane is obviously a huge turn-off," she quips with a dramatic sigh.

"Obviously," I agree.

"And this location is terrible."

"Awful."

"In fact, you probably owe me multiple favors now."

"Just let me know," I say, giving her a slow glance.

She looks away and the car is quiet for a few minutes. I think Chloe is thinking, or enjoying the view. It's hard to tell. I take the next exit onto Grand Avenue, then a right onto Broadway and park in front of a small log cabin-inspired building.

"Are we here?" Chloe leans forward and looks out the window while unbuckling her seat belt.

"No, Vail is another thirty minutes. I thought we'd stop for breakfast."

We grab a table inside and Chloe looks over the menu while I look over her. I've been here at least a dozen times. The Red Canyon Cafe is my favorite stop for breakfast if I have an early flight. The waitress fills our coffee while Chloe fidgets and reads the menu over again. Finally she speaks.

"Knock, knock."

"Why are you nervous?" She only whips out the jokes when she's nervous.

"I don't know." She shrugs. "This is weird."

"What's weird?"

"Um…" She wrinkles her nose and gestures between us with her hand. "This. Us traveling together. Being your fake girlfriend today. It's all weird." She dumps a packet of fake sweetener into her coffee and then fiddles with the empty wrapper, tearing it into tiny pieces before wadding them together into a snowball.

"You worry too much," I note.

"You think?" she replies drily.

"So who's at the door?"

She looks over to the restaurant door then back to me, a flicker of confusion crossing her face before she laughs. "We have to start over! Knock, knock."

"Who's there?"

"Butter."

"Butter who?"

"I butter tell you a few more knock-knock jokes!" Then she peals into a fit of laughter. I rest my elbow on the table and watch her. I love the way her eyes sparkle when she's amused. "Oh, that reminds me, I just read this book where the guy used butter—" She stops short. "Never mind." She waves her hand. "Want to hear another joke?"

I tilt my head and wonder why she stopped. "The guy used butter for what? To kill someone?" I guess, knowing her love of murder mysteries.

She blinks then agrees. "Yup. That's what he did. Anyway, want to hear another joke?" She's really interested in moving on from the butter, which just piques my interest even more.

"How?"

"What?" She blinks like a deer in the headlights.

"How did he kill someone with butter?"

She pauses too long so I already know she's about to lie. "Um…" Her eyes flicker to the window. "I forgot."

"You forgot?"

"Yeah." She shakes her head and picks up the sweetener packet snowball she made earlier and rolls it between her finger and thumb. "I don't remember."

"Huh," I reply and stare at her for a few moments while I think about that. "What kind of book was it?" I ask and her eyes widen. Bingo. "Was it a murder-mystery book, Chloe?" I ask just to fuck with her. "Or maybe a cookbook?" I'm completely straight-faced. "Were you looking up a pound cake recipe? Lots of butter in pound cake." I trail off and rub my jaw. "Or... wait. Was it a filthy romance novel?" I fake stupefaction. "Were they using butter to do dirty sexual things? Chloe Scott, I am shocked. Shocked. You teach the second grade." I shake my head in mock disappointment. "I can't believe you would fill your head with such filth."

The waitress stops by to take our orders and refill our coffees. I tell her Chloe wants extra butter with breakfast while Chloe groans and slaps her palm against her forehead. When the waitress leaves Chloe rolls her eyes at me and asks if I'm done or if she needs to put me in the timeout corner, which just makes me grin.

"Tell me more about the timeout corner, Miss Scott. I might be interested."

"Hey, can I tell you a joke about pizza?" she responds, apparently ready to change the subject.

"Okay." I nod.

"Forget it—you'll think it's cheesy." She grins. "Get it? Cheesy!"

"You must be very popular at school."

"I do okay," she says, but she smiles shyly and shrugs.

**

After breakfast we continue towards Vail, getting back onto Highway 6 before quickly merging onto I-70. We'll be in Vail Village in under half an hour. The highway isn't straight here. The road curves through the canyon, following the path of least resistance as it was constructed. It makes for an impressive view with which Chloe is enamored. I can't blame her. Vail Village in the fall is something to see. I don't usually visit until there's enough snow for skiing, but maybe I'll start. Chloe is hypnotized over the colors of the trees and the sheer size of it all and I'm captivated by watching her enjoy it.

We're turning onto Frontage Road headed into Vail Village when she tells me she met someone.

"What's that?" I ask, trying to keep the irritation out of my voice.

She nods and pulls out her phone. "On Facebook. I don't know why I'm bothering with dating sites when there are guys like this available." She waves the phone.

Fuck that. I'm available.

"I don't think you're ready yet," I snap. "We're still practicing your dating skills, remember?"

"Oh." She frowns. "Are we exclusively practicing? I didn't know. I thought this guy would be good practice."

I make a mental note to hack her and alter all the incoming messages from men. Why the hell didn't I do this the day I met her? When she told me about men sending her photos of their dicks?

"So tell me about him," I finally say. I might as well get his name so I can delete his shit first.

"His name is Tom," she gushes, "and he really wants to meet me."

"Uh-huh."

"But first he needs me to send him money for airfare. That sounds reasonable, don't you think?"

"No." I frown as I take a right onto Lionshead Circle. I'm putting an end to this today and I'm feeling pretty satisfied that I had the foresight to pack my laptop. Bye-bye, Tom.

"Well, Tom is ready to make a commitment. He is"—
she glances at the phone—"much impressed with me and
would like to proceed our courtship. I think he might be
a keeper because he doesn't even care that I'm pregnant
with your baby."

Jesus fuck. She's messing with me.

"He said"—she scrolls through the messages on her
phone before continuing—"These are the things that
happen and we must all love the babies.'"

"Chloe," I groan.

"Then I asked him if he liked long walks on the beach
and he asked me for my age date."

I pull into the valet at the Arrabelle and put the car
into park before looking at Chloe.

"So what do you think?" she asks, eyes wide. "I mean
obviously we have a little language barrier to work out,
but I think he has potential."

I snatch the phone from her hand and tap out a quick
'fuck off' to Tom before blocking him from Chloe's
account and passing the phone back.

"Hey!" she protests, but she's laughing. Little imp.

"Why would you even reply to that guy, Chloe?"

"I don't get out much, Boyd. I gotta practice where I
can."

"You don't need any practice being a smartass."

"Boyd Gallagher." She lowers her lashes and gives me
a seductive glance. "That might be the nicest thing you've
ever said to me." Then she laughs.

Thirteen

Chloe

Holy wow. I'm in Vail with Boyd. For the weekend. The entire freaking weekend! Why did I agree to this? I never should have agreed to this. He caught me off guard, showing up at my apartment last night. It never occurred to me that the wedding would be anywhere other than Philadelphia and then when he showed and told me to pack a bag I couldn't think fast enough of any reasonable reason not to go.

I'm not cool enough to pull off this fake girlfriend stuff for an entire weekend. I'm not a very good liar and besides that, I find him really attractive. Which should make it easier to fake, but it just makes it harder because I get all flustered and start telling stupid jokes.

This hotel is incredible. We're not even past the lobby and I already know I've never stayed anywhere this nice. The flooring is a sort of cobblestone, which my suitcase would be bumping across right now if I had my suitcase. "They'll send them up," Boyd said, like it was no big deal. I guess it's not if you're used to that sort of thing.

We bypass the front desk and exit through a glass door into a courtyard centered by a fountain. The view is a little like being in the midst of a Disney fairytale come to life. Brick pavers line the ground, the sun is shining and I'm positive I just heard a bird chirp. The architecture makes me feel like I've been transported to an Alpine village somewhere in Europe. The slope of the roofs, the arched doorways, the stone construction and elaborate wooden terraces all combine to make the town look a century older than it can possibly be. It's magic. On the other side of the courtyard we re-enter through another set of glass doors and walk across another cobblestone floor until we reach the hotel spa.

Where Boyd promptly leaves me. I don't know how, but one minute he's there and the next minute I'm being led into a fancy changing room by Hilda and given a fluffy robe to wear. By the time I get a massage good enough to make me forget why I'm here and my fingers and toes have been painted, my dress and shoes have materialized. But they're not done with me. My hair and makeup are taken care of as well and now I really do feel like I'm in the midst of a Disney movie.

And then Boyd is there. In a tux. And somehow I manage to have a dozen dirty thoughts about him in under ten seconds, which makes my cheeks flush and my heart race. I start to get nervous but then I remind myself that this is fake—there's no need to be nervous. But oh, holy wow. Boyd's hotness isn't fake, that's for sure.

"I didn't think about a wrap for you," Boyd says, slipping his jacket off and putting it over my shoulders as we step outside into the cobblestone courtyard. He takes my hand and guides me out of the courtyard and along another fairytale-inspired walkway lined with shops and restaurants. When we reach the end of the walkway the view of Vail Mountain spreads before us and I realize we're headed to the gondola.

"Are we going up?" I ask, bouncing a little in excitement.

"Just for the ceremony. The reception is back at the hotel." He grins, seemingly amused with my excitement.

We get a gondola to ourselves and sit side by side facing the top of the mountain as we ascend. When I turn to look at Boyd I'm not sure if it's him or the mountain backdrop behind him that threatens to take my breath away. And then I wonder what the mountain looks like covered in snow—and how much time Boyd spends here in the winter with how many different women.

The ceremony is as stunning as you'd expect it to be in that location, the group relatively small. It's Boyd's cousin Amy getting married, I learn. I spot a slide as we're walking back to the gondola after the ceremony. A freaking slide, on a mountain. Boyd laughs as my steps slow a bit while I try to get a look at it. "I'll take you tomorrow," he promises.

At the reception I meet several members of his family. He introduces me to everyone as his girlfriend and his hands are constantly on me, not in a disrespectful way, but in a very comfortable way. I feel his hand lightly on my back as we walk, on my hip pulling me closer to him as we stand. When we sit he drapes his arm across the back of my chair and brushes his fingertips over my upper arm.

And I don't have to freak out about any of it, worry about what any of it means or if I'm going to embarrass myself. I don't have to be afraid of these people not liking me or judging me, because it's all fake. I'm simply here as a favor to Boyd. So I relax and lean my head on his shoulder. I snuggle in next to him at every opportunity because it feels good. Whatever this is, it feels good.

When his great-aunt comments about what adorable babies Boyd and I would make, I don't freak out and start telling jokes. I simply nod in agreement and hold up my empty ring finger and respond, "First things first," with a sweet smile on my face. I'm feeling pretty smug about putting Boyd on the spot in retaliation for this charade, but he doesn't look bothered in the least. He replies with some quip about teaching the kids to ski.

Being a fake girlfriend is the best gig ever.

I don't have to stress about anything. Am I boring him? Who cares, this isn't a real date. Will his family like me? Who cares, I'll never see them again! Will I run out of things to talk about? Does he think I'm weird? Is he having a good time? Does he secretly care that I just ate both of our desserts? None of it matters because we're just pretending!

When I meet his mother, whose attempt at small talk is coldly sizing me up and asking me to tell her what I like about her son, I guilelessly place my hand on Boyd's chest and tilt my head to rest on his shoulder. Which as a side note was probably a huge tactical error, because the feel of Boyd's chest under my hand is distracting. But I manage to persevere.

"How long do you have, Mrs. Gallagher?" I beam at the woman while sliding my other hand behind Boyd's back. Damn, that's a mistake too. How much time does this guy spend in the gym?

"Excuse me?" Mrs. Gallagher replies, clearly not understanding where I'm going with this.

"It would take me all evening to tell you everything I love about Boyd, so I was just wondering how much time you had?" I turn my gaze to Boyd midway through speaking to his mom and my heart falters for a minute because I realize that even though I'm fake-gushing to his mom, all of the examples that spring to mind of what I like about Boyd are completely one hundred percent true.

Like the way that he looks at me. And how he always holds open the door open for me, even when he's just arrested my date or he's taking me shopping for a wedding he's manipulated me into attending with him. I like the way he kissed me last week without overwhelming me. The way he teases me about my obsession with crime and safety. I like his eyelashes. And most of all I like how patient he is with me.

And when he looks back at me it doesn't feel like he's pretending either. He closes the gap between us and kisses me, right in the middle of his cousin's wedding reception. It's not a peck and it's not the aggressive kiss from last weekend against my front door. It's soft and just long enough to make my stomach drop and my pulse hike into overdrive. And a moment later it's over and I'm confused. Hot, bothered and confused.

We dance and eat and have a few drinks until I'm yawning and resting my head on Boyd's shoulder and he kisses the top of my head and says we can leave. I'm in a hazy cloud of contentment that lasts until we reach the hotel room—the hotel room that I've yet to see. It starts to fade as the alcohol wears off and Boyd inserts the key into the door. By the time the electronic lock blinks green my anxiety is starting to creep back in. The fake girlfriend part of the evening is over.

The room is stunning, of course. The curtains are open, showcasing the view of the mountain, and there's a lit fireplace in the corner. These details distract me for approximately three seconds from the real issue with this room.

"Knock, knock, Boyd."

"Who's there, Chloe?" He looks amused, and hotter than should be legal as he undoes his tie.

"One bed! One bed is here, that's who." I don't realize

I've stomped my foot in emphasis until I catch Boyd's gaze traveling down my leg. Then he laughs while slipping the cufflinks out of his shirt and rolling the sleeves back while my nerves skyrocket. What am I doing here? How did I allow this to happen? My brief experiences with sex never included an overnight—they included getting home by curfew or retreating back to my own dorm room when it was over. And while I don't think Boyd wants to have sex with me, spending the night with him in the same bed is almost as nerve-racking.

"Sorry," he says, glancing at me. "This was the only room they had left. I can sleep on the couch if that would make you more comfortable?"

I glance at the couch and feel stupid. "Of course not, it's fine."

He watches me for another moment attentively then nods. "You can change in the bathroom. Your suitcase is on a stand in the wardrobe," he tells me, nodding at the furniture behind me.

I open the doors and dig into my suitcase, still gnawing on my lip when I feel him behind me. "Do you need help with the zipper?" he asks.

Yes. Yes, I do need help with the zipper. I nod and he unzips a very modest length before telling me I should able to get it from there. His voice is soft but husky and I don't want to get it from there. I want him to yank the dress from my body and fuck me against the wall, but I don't know how to ask for that. I barely know how to be alone with him.

I take refuge in the bathroom and close the double doors behind me. Apparently just one door isn't enough for a fancy bathroom in a five-star hotel. I don't see any obvious way to lock it though, so I settle for shutting the doors firmly so they won't spring open before washing my makeup off and brushing my teeth. Then I yank on the lavender cotton sleep shorts and gray long-sleeved waffle-knit tee I brought to sleep in and remove the pins from my hair while running my fingers through it.

Okay then. I tap my fingers on my thigh and examine myself in the mirror. *Just go back out there and go to bed. That's all you have to do. No big deal. He might even be asleep already.* I blow out a breath at my reflection and then scoop the dress off the floor and exit the bathroom. I stop at the wardrobe to slip the dress onto a hanger, then close the doors and turn towards the room.

"Holy shit, are you naked?" I blurt out. Boyd's sitting in the bed with the covers up to his waist, his back against the headboard reading something on his tablet. His chest is bare, his perfect, six-pack abs assaulting my eyes from less than ten feet away. This isn't fair, I mean come on.

"No," he says slowly. I think he's confused by me, but I'm not sure because his eyes are on my bare legs and he's not saying anything. I want to tug at the hem of these sleep shorts, but I resist and instead mentally chastise myself for not packing sweatpants. He flips the cover back and points at his legs—covered by pajama pants.

I'm an idiot. My cheeks flush as I get into the other side of the bed and lie down on my side, facing the wall.

"Just to clarify, you have seen a penis, right?" Boyd asks, the hint of laughter in his voice.

"Oh, my God. Shut up!" I slap a hand over my eyes like that might suddenly transport me out of this mess and back to my own apartment. It doesn't. "I already told you that I have, but I haven't seen yours, okay? I'm sure yours is super special." I'm going to die of awkward. I cannot look at him, I cannot.

"Well, thank you, Chloe. I like to think that it is."

There's no hint of laughter in his voice now. Because he's flat-out laughing. "Good night, Chloe."

"Good night, Boyd."

FOURTEEN
BOYD

This was a bad idea. This trip. This hotel room. The one bed. Bad, all bad. Sometime during the night her back ended up cuddled to my front, her ass lined up with my cock. Spooning. We're fucking spooning.

The texture of her shirt is pressed against my bare chest and I know logically that waffle-weave cotton is the least sexy thing on the planet, but my dick hasn't gotten the message. I've somehow managed to sling an arm around her as she slept and her legs are pressed against mine. Knowing they're bare just past her tiny excuse for shorts is killing me. Then she shifts and her toes nudge my shin—and my balls get bluer than they already are. I woke up a few minutes ago with a hard-on that got progressively worse as I remembered where I was and who I was pressed up against. Her hair still manages to smell faintly like vanilla and strawberry even with the remnants of hair spray from yesterday. And it's soft. I know this because I'm playing with the strands flung across my pillow. Like a pervert. Or a besotted asshole.

I hope I've read her right. I hope this plan I've contrived to get what I want works. Or I'm fucked. I detach myself from her and roll out of bed. She murmurs and her eyelids flutter before she rolls to her back and stretches. I need a shower, right now.

I stand under the hot water for what feels like an hour, my hand wrapped around my cock providing about as much satisfaction as fake-dating Chloe does. Don't get me wrong, I jerk off and I enjoy it. But masturbation never compares with the real thing. Ever. It's like the difference between watching the NFL on TV and being on the field. And my dick is more than ready to suit up and get in the game with Chloe.

I step out of the bathroom with a towel wrapped around my waist. I didn't think about clothing on my way in, too preoccupied to think that far ahead.

"Finally!" Chloe says when the bathroom door opens. "Why were you in the shower for thirty-five minutes?" she asks as I round the corner to grab clean clothing from my suitcase. "I mean, there's a water shortage in the Mountain States, Boyd…" She trails off when she realizes I'm naked save for the towel.

"Don't ask questions you don't want the answers to," I respond sardonically and step back into the bathroom to dress.

Chloe's quiet when I return. She's sitting in the middle of the bed, legs bent with her arms wrapped around them, staring at me. There's entirely too much of her legs exposed for my liking so I tell her to take a shower because I'm not quite sure how to tell her to put on some goddamned pants without sounding like a dick.

By the time she emerges from the bathroom dressed, hair still wet and tousled, I've had room service delivered. "Sorry, they didn't have donuts," I tell her, indicating the food set up on the table. "I got you a waffle with Nutella."

She slows from putting something into her suitcase and looks at me, suspicious. "You remembered I like Nutella?"

"I'm a pretty amazing boyfriend," I say and pull out a chair for her. She looks at me a second longer before sitting.

"So are we still pretending today?" she asks, not looking at me so I can't gauge her exact meaning. Are we still pretending that I need a fake girlfriend? Are we still pretending that I didn't set this entire thing up so that I could spend time with her without her being anxious about it being real? Or is she asking if we're still pretending for show? I take a sip of coffee and watch her while she slices the waffle and stuffs a piece in her mouth. She raises her eyebrows while she chews, as if to question why I'm not answering her.

"I don't know, what do you want to do today?" *Nice deflection, Boyd.*

She rolls her eyes as she swallows. "I meant do we have to do any wedding stuff today?" She tears off the end of a sweetener packet and dumps it into an empty mug. "Will we see anyone?"

Okay then.

I pick up the carafe and fill her mug and watch while she adds cream and swirls it with a spoon before sipping. "Uh, I don't think so. Maybe. I'm not sure when everyone is leaving town. But no, we don't have to do anything today. Except the slide. We have to do the slide."

"Really?" Her eyes light up.

"Of course. I told you yesterday I'd take you back. Have I steered you wrong yet? Have a little faith, Chloe."

"Hmm, well, other than blackmailing me, no, you haven't steered me wrong."

"Smartass."

She takes another bite of waffle and eyes me. I can see her gaze lingering on my arms as I take a spoonful of oatmeal.

"We can go after breakfast?" she finally asks, an obvious frown of doubt on her face.

I nod, not sure where she's going with this.

"Are you sure?" she asks playfully. "You don't need to hit the gym first?" she presses. "I've seen you half naked and that body does not happen without a lot of maintenance," she teases.

"Oh, this?" I lean back and glance down at my shirt-covered torso then back to her. "I maintain this with sex. Nothing but sex."

Her eyes go wide. She clearly wasn't expecting that response. She tilts her head a fraction and the skin on her forehead wrinkles in concentration. "Really?"

Jesus, this girl. "No." I shake my head with a laugh. "I work out plenty," I tell her. "But I'm glad you approve," I add with a lift of my eyebrow.

We leave the Arrabelle and retrace our steps from yesterday to the gondola, Chloe chattering the entire way. She asks about various relatives she met last night. Comments about how beautiful the bride looked and how enchanting the venue was. She's not telling jokes, so while she seems a little nervous, I think she's okay.

We have to stop and get lift tickets and sign a release today. Yesterday it was pre-arranged as part of the wedding. I grab a form and dash off a signature then turn towards the counter to pay when I realize Chloe is still reading the form. Line by line. She catches me staring at her and glances at my form.

"You already signed it? Without reading it?" She's appalled. "This is a legal document, Boyd," she says, jabbing a finger onto the paper in front of her.

"It's just a slide, Chloe. Not a death trap."

She glares at me and then goes back to carefully

reading the form while I watch, amused as hell. Finally she frowns and, with a tiny shake of her head and a small sigh, signs the form.

"Are you satisfied now, safety girl? Are you fully prepared for the slide of death?"

"At least one of us is," she retorts.

I buy the lift tickets and then we cross over to the gondola. She's got her phone with her today and she starts snapping pictures as soon as we get in and doesn't stop until we exit at the top. It's a perfect clear view today, but then it almost always is. Chilly air and bright fluffy white clouds set the scene as Chloe twirls—actually twirls like she's reenacting a scene from *The Sound of Music*. But instead of singing she's taking more pictures.

"What are you going to do with these pics?" I ask her as we walk down the path towards the Forest Flyer.

"What do you mean?"

"You didn't tell anyone we were coming here."

"I didn't know we were coming here," she deadpans, then pauses. "That's weird that I didn't tell anyone. You've lulled me into a false sense of security, Agent Gallagher."

"False? Do you think you're in danger with me?"

"Oh, true. I suppose I'm not. But on my TV shows they never say, 'The victim was lulled into a safe and secure location and lived happily ever after.'"

"You're ridiculous."

"A little," she agrees with a nod. "I guess I'll have to keep them for myself," she says a little sadly. "But this view is too pretty not to capture."

There's a group of young boys ahead of us at the Forest Flyer. I nudge Chloe in the ribs and nod my head towards the kids. "Look, Chlo. If the slide is safe for children it's probably safe for you too."

"Shut up."

I scan over the sled setup as one of the employees recites off the safety instructions and then I ask Chloe how much she weighs.

"Excuse me?" She stops dead and stares at me like I'm a monster.

"We can ride together."

"I don't think so." She's shaking her head.

"Sure we can. You can't possibly weigh more than one fifteen. We're well below the weight limit for one sled." Her eyes bug out, but I grab her hand and tug her along to the loading zone anyway. The sled is designed to hold one or two people and grips a metal track a few feet above the ground. I easily throw my leg over and sit then pat the empty wedge of a space in front of me for the second rider. "Hop on."

Begrudgingly she does. The height is too high for her so she places a hand on my shoulder and steps onto the sled before turning and dropping her bottom into the seat. Yeah, maybe this was a bad idea. Her legs are tucked between mine and when I press the side handles allowing the sled to slide or slowing it down, my chest and arms are damn near wrapped around her. The workers make sure our seat belts are fastened and reiterate the distance we need to keep between sleds and then we're flying three thousand four hundred feet down the side of the mountain, curving around trees and over drops. But she laughs the entire way down so the ache in my balls from having her pressed against me is worth it.

The slide is designed to pull the rider back to the top so the exit and entrance are at the same place. But when we reach the gate house Chloe wiggles in her seat and says, "Again!"

"Again? What are you, eight?"

"Shut up," she replies happily and tilts her head back to smile at me upside down. We take two more runs down the mountain before she's satiated.

We walk around the top of Vail Mountain until Chloe gets bored taking pictures and after I manage to photobomb a couple of the selfies she tries to take. She finally hands me her phone and I take one of the two of us and then text it to myself from her phone.

After taking the gondola back down the mountain we wander around the village, ducking into and out of stores as we walk. The chocolate shop interests her but not much else. Mostly she likes to look. She does pick up a t-shirt in one store and as she's heading to the cashier with it I ask her what she's doing.

"It's t-shirt day at school on Friday," she says.

I look at the shirt and then back to her, raising my eyebrow at her in disbelief.

She glances at it again and shakes her head. "It's a bad idea, huh? I was going to wear it to school, but I'd probably forget and wear it in front of Everly and then she'd be all, 'Chloe, when were you in Colorado?' and then I'd have to lie and yeah, that's just a mess."

"Not what I was thinking," I tell her.

"Oh. Were you thinking I should just tell her I came with you to Colorado?" She tilts her head back to look at me, her expression serious, and I'm totally confused about where she's going with this but I don't have time to think about it because I start to laugh.

"Chloe, what do you think that shirt means?"

She makes a disgusted face at my laughter and shakes the shirt in the air. "It's a highway sign, Boyd." She says it like I'm crazy. "The 420. See? All the highway signs in this country have the same shape. Or maybe it's an interstate sign. Is there a difference?"

"And you think the 420 is a highway?"

"Uh, yeah. It's probably that highway we took to get here from the airport," she says. And then she nods at herself. "Probably, since they've got all this stuff with the 420 on it."

I can't help it. I start laughing.

"What?" She looks confused.

"The 420 highway does not exist. It's a pot reference."

"No, it's not." She starts to laugh but stops. "Really?"

"Really."

The blood drains from her face as she politely refolds the shirt and places it back on the stack she got it from. Then she straightens her back and walks primly out of the store. She starts laughing as soon as she hits the sidewalk.

"I would have been suspended by lunch." She's laughing so hard she has to bend over. "How is that a pot reference? Why is it on a highway sign?" Then she crosses her legs and announces she's gonna pee if she laughs any harder as she falls sideways into me.

I grab onto her so she doesn't topple to the ground and then, fuck it. I kiss her. Her legs are still twisted and she's off balance with her chest pressed against mine. She makes a squeak of surprise that quickly turns into the softest moan I've ever heard and then her hands are on my shoulders. I have a moment of apprehension that she's going to push me away but it vanishes when her fingers tentatively wrap behind my neck, because she's not pushing—she's pulling me closer. I keep one arm wrapped around her for support while moving the other hand into her hair. Which allows me to do what I've wanted to do since the first time I saw her—wind it around my hand to maneuver her soft pink lips exactly where I want them. Well, no, not exactly where I want them—not with an audience.

I move my lips down to her jaw. This kiss is the best of my life. Every kiss with Chloe is the best kiss of my life, but this one, fuck. This one will be hard to top. Better than against her doorway when I shocked the hell out of her. Better than at the wedding when I wasn't entirely sure she wasn't just playing along. Her thumbs are rubbing little circles into the skin just above the collar of my shirt and the soft sighs and low moans coming out of her are driving me wild. And God help me, somewhere in all this she's managed to unwind her legs and hike one of them around my thigh, trying to grind herself against me.

She breaks away, her breathing shallow, and meets my eyes.

"I'm hungry."

Yes.

"Can we get pizza?" she asks, pointing to a sign about twenty yards away. "I think we should get pizza." And then she starts walking.

Wait. We're getting pizza?

What the fuck just happened?

Fifteen

Chloe

What the heck just happened? I think I just tried to dry-hump Boyd's thigh in public. We were laughing and then we were kissing and then my slutty leg went rogue and now we're having pizza. Pizza is good.

"Blue Moose Pizza," I read off the sign as we approach the restaurant. "What a funny name, don't you think? Moose aren't blue. Unless you're high on pot, right?" I glance quickly at Boyd then away again. "I think. I mean, I've never actually been high. Does it work like that? Never mind, it doesn't matter. Pizza!" I grab the door and dash inside.

Inside, we're seated at a red-and-white checkered table and given menus. Boyd orders a beer and I order a Moosarita. For real, that's what it's called. Then I bury my face in the menu while Boyd stares at me from across the table.

"What kind of pizza do you want?" I ask him.

"Whatever you want," he responds.

"Buffalo wing pizza?" I ask, still not looking up.

"Fine," he agrees and places the order as the waitress drops off our drinks.

With the orders placed and menus gone, I've run out of distractions so I look at him. He looks like he wants to devour me. Pizza was a stupid idea. I should have taken him straight back to our room. What is wrong with me? Freaking social anxiety.

"So," Boyd starts and I wet my lips with my tongue and run my eyes over him. He's so... everything. He's wearing a lightweight sweater and he's pushed the sleeves up to his elbows. I love his arms. And his shoulders. And pretty much every bit of him that I've felt so far. I bet he's hung like a horse. No, a moose! I bite my lip to keep from laughing at my own mental joke. Then I frown. What if he's really huge? I've seen a total of three penises, not counting all the POD's I've been sent and they were all sort of similar. You know, different but the same? Like the one curved a little more than the other two—

"Chloe?" Boyd interrupts my thoughts and I suspect he might have been trying to get my attention for a while.

"What?" I like his fingertips too, the way they rest against the beer bottle. His index finger rubbing at a corner of the label that's pulling away from the bottle is turning me on. Big time. Big, big. I shake my head and laugh.

I want to have sex with Boyd Gallagher.

I have no idea how to make that happen. Not really. Was I supposed to say something after that kiss? It was just a kiss. A really hot panty-wetting kiss, but still. It's not an invitation. It doesn't mean he wants to have sex with me. Or does it? Guys are pretty transparent, right? But Boyd isn't my high-school boyfriend, who I knew was just waiting for me to give the okay. Boyd isn't one of the two lanky college boys I played awkward encounter with in semi-lit dorm rooms.

Boyd is... Boyd. He all but admitted he could have brought a casual date with him to Vail, but it wasn't worth the hassle of the woman thinking it meant something. So I don't think Boyd is desperate to have sex with some random horny girl. He must have plenty of options. Easier options than me. Options with savvy sex skills.

Should I bring it up now? 'Hey, Boyd, would you like to have sex with me? Perhaps after dinner?' I tap my fingers on my thigh and realize that my leg is bouncing under the table. *Calm down, Chloe.* He does seem to be into teaching me though. Maybe I should tell him I need the practice? That's not even a lie. I do need the practice. My sex skills are not savvy. I wonder if that's a weird request? I mean, obviously it's totally weird. But I wonder if he would mind?

"Chloe," Boyd interrupt again. "What are you thinking about?"

"The 420," I say without missing a beat. Apparently my lying skills are on point. "Are you positive about the 420 thing? I really think the 420 is a highway."

"That's what you're thinking about right now?" he asks quietly, leaning forward a little and pinning me with his eyes.

"Yup. I'm gonna look it up. I love to look things up. Did you know that? Google is my jam." I whip my phone out and start tapping. I think I hear Boyd grunt before he takes a sip of beer.

Chloe: Random question. Did you ever have a sex teacher?

Everly: Ohhh, like a dirty student-teacher situation?

Chloe: No, not like that.

Everly: Are you going to have sex with a teacher? I

don't know if that counts as teacher sex now that you're no longer a student, but you should still go for it. You can always roleplay if that's what does it for you.

Chloe: Not what I meant!!!!

Everly: No, I never fucked a teacher. Sad. I wonder if I can interest Sawyer in playing naughty schoolgirl with me?

Chloe: I don't think we're talking about the same thing.

Everly: ...

I stare at the little dots that tell me she's typing but then they stop. I can almost guarantee she's shopping for a schoolgirl getup and has forgotten about me.

Chloe: HELLO?

Everly: Sorry. Do you know how many options there are for sexy schoolgirl on the internet? Do you think I'm tall enough to pull off knee-high socks without looking stupid? My legs are not that long.

"Find anything?" Boyd asks and I almost jump in my seat.

"Um..." I stall while I abandon my text message with Everly and do a quick search on Interstate 420. "According to Wikipedia, Interstate 420 refers to two highways that were never built. In Georgia and Louisiana. So almost a highway?" I offer with a quick glance in his direction and then back at my phone as I try a new search without the word 'interstate.' "Yeah, it means pot all right." I shake my head. "You are correct."

Everly: So what did you think of Boyd?

Oh, shit.

Chloe: What are you talking about?

Everly: Boyd? Sophie's brother? Sophie's incredibly hot brother?

Chloe: Why are you asking?

Everly: Why am I asking? What kind of evasive question is that? Because you finally met him when Christine was born and I think you should go out with him and have his babies. That's why I'm asking.

Chloe: Oh, right.

Everly: Pretty sure he could teach you anything you want to know.......

Chloe: Just got a pizza delivered. Gotta go.

The waitress is coming with the pizza, so it's not really lying. I set the phone down on the booth seat beside me as the waitress sets the pizza in the middle of the table and asks if we need anything else before leaving us alone.
"Today was fun. Thank you."
"Fun?"
"The slide and stuff."

"You're welcome." He takes another sip of his beer and watches me so I slide a slice onto my plate and start imagining what Boyd is like in bed. Normal, right? That reminds me about his penis. I need to look this up right now. I'll feel better if I have all the variables ahead of time. Being prepared for every eventuality makes me feel better.

I take a bite of pizza and then slip my phone off the bench and do a quick search on average penis size. Which actually, as it turns out, isn't that helpful because there's two million search results. I need a chart. I find one and glance from it to Boyd and back again. I'm not sure what I think I'm going to determine from staring at him across the table and looking at a chart at the internet. This is so stupid. I'm stupid. It's not like I haven't had sex before. I'm making myself anxious over nothing, because this is what I do.

"What are you looking at?"

"Um, the internet?" I respond and shove the phone in my pocket. "Sorry, I just needed to check on something real quick."

"Okay."

"Hey, have you ever sent anyone a POD?"

He doesn't respond to that, simply lowers his chin an inch and raises his eyebrows in question.

"A dick pic," I say, lowering my voice.

"I grew up as the son of a politician with countless lectures about the implications of what I put on the internet and I made my career specializing in cyber crimes for federal government. I can assure you, I have never sent a dick pic."

"Oh." I nod. "That makes sense."

He just stares at me for another moment while I take a sip of my Moosarita.

"Are you upset that I kissed you?"

"No." I shake my head back and forth. "No."

"Okay." He says it slowly like he's not sure he believes me.

"I'm not upset."

"Okay." This time he says it without question.

"I liked it," I insist. "My leg liked it a lot." This moment is weird. There's all this weird energy between us. Or maybe it's all in my head? How does anyone know? I want to toss some cash on the table and drag him back to our hotel room, but maybe he's questioning why he brought me on this trip when he could have brought someone—anyone—else.

But he laughs and says, "My leg liked it too, Chloe," so I think maybe we're on the same page.

Sixteen

Chloe

When we get back to the hotel I grab my pajamas and disappear into the bathroom. Because I need to put my pajamas on before sex? Are we even having the sex? I wonder what he's doing out there. How long have I been in this bathroom? Great, now he probably thinks I have stomach issues on top of being the official leader of Team Awkward. I slap my palm against my forehead and stare at myself in the bathroom mirror. *Be normal, Chloe. You got this.*

I place my hand on the door handle and take a deep breath. Then I drop my hand. Boyd is going to expect more than those college guys did. Like what if he tries to bend me into some weird position I don't know about and I embarrass myself? What if he wants me on top? I can probably figure that out. What if he wants to stick it in my ass? Wait, I'm sort of open to that actually. Maybe. I think I'd be open to anything Boyd wanted to do together. He's always very conscientious with me, I can't imagine that's going to disappear during sex.

If we're having sex, that is.

I find him at the desk, still dressed and tapping away on his laptop. The fireplace is lit, but I'm honestly not sure it hasn't been running since we got here so I have no idea if he did it. The curtains are thankfully closed and only the desk lamp and the light near the door are on.

All right, let's do this. I clear my throat and then speak.

"We can do this the easy way, or the fun way."

"What does that mean exactly?" He stops typing and looks at me over the open laptop, amused bewilderment crossing his face.

"I have no idea. I just wanted to say it."

He closes the laptop and fixes his gaze on me, silent.

"What do you call a moose that plays a musical instrument?" I babble.

He silently shakes his head no, while raising his hand and beckoning, indicating I should come closer without saying a word. When I stop a couple of feet in front of him he stands and closes the distance between us, stopping when we're toe to toe. He nudges my chin with his finger so I have to look up at him. He looks... he looks like he's into me. So this is happening. I'm gonna have sex with Boyd.

And then I start giggling.

In my defense this moment is really tense. I mean, no, it's not tense. It's serious. And I can't really deal with serious moments. I can at work. Parent-teacher conferences? No problem. Resolving a dispute between second-graders that has no basis in logic? Easy peasy. I'm not nervous at work. I'm in my element at work. But now? Not so much.

But then Boyd cups my ass and lifts me and my legs wrap around him like they've done it a hundred times before and I stop laughing. Adrenaline takes over and adrenaline is a heck of a lot more compelling than doubt.

Then he turns us around and backs me against the wall, his lips descending on mine while I run my fingers into his hair and tug.

"Why are you so patient with me?" I ask.

"Because I like you."

"Oh," I whisper. "Okay."

"I want to take your clothes off, Chloe," he murmurs while nipping my ear lobe between his teeth.

I nod. "Me too. I want that too," I agree and drop my hands to the hem of my tee and wiggle it up between us and over my head. It hits the carpet with an almost inaudible whoosh. "You too, I want your shirt off too." I tug at his sweater until he leans back just enough and takes over, casting it over his head.

I flatten my palms against him and explore, pressing the heels of my hands against him firmly while my fingertips are gentle in their analysis.

"You're so beautiful, Chloe." He says it with a husky edge to his voice while running his own hands up my sides until he reaches my breasts, then cups them with his palms. When he rolls my nipples between finger and thumb my head falls back and hits the wall while I grind my pelvis closer to him, my body instinctively seeking more. "Do you understand? Do you have any idea?"

"What?" My hands have moved to his biceps and I'm tracing the muscles there with my fingertips as I work my way towards his shoulders.

"How beautiful you are? How much you drive me crazy?"

"I want you to take off your pants," I breathe into his ear and I can feel the smile stretch across his face.

"Good. I want that too," he says, repeating my earlier words with a smile in his tone.

I'm feeling warm everywhere, like being a little drunk without actually being a little drunk. And I feel excited about whatever is about to happen. Because I know it's going to be good. He moves his hands back to my bottom to support me as he carries me to the bed and sets me on the edge.

My hands immediately move to the button on his jeans and I unfasten it then work the zipper down before giving the denim a little tug near his hips to free him from the pants. He's wearing briefs underneath and they do nothing to hide the size of his erection. I flick my eyes up to his and lick my lips as I snake my hand inside his briefs to grasp him. I'm about to congratulate myself for my amazing poker face, except Boyd is laughing at me so I guess I didn't quite pull off the sophisticated reaction I was going for.

He finishes the job of undressing and I take a quick inventory of him from head to toe. Adonis doesn't even come close. He's firm and toned everywhere. Every-freaking-where. I wrap my hand around the length of him and stroke back and forth a few times. I feel myself getting wet just from the simple act of touching him, my body's instinctive desire to ease the path for the size of him.

Because yeah, it's definitely the model for the large penis on the size chart.

"We're not doing anal," I inform him. "Not with this," I add, stroking him up to the tip and exploring the broad head with my thumb. He's thick and veined and hard against my palm.

He blows out a breath in a hiss and covers my hand with his own, tightening my grip considerably before pausing. "Wait, was anal on the table?"

"I'm really curious about it," I admit, "but not with that thing." I nod at his monster dick.

"The burden I bear," he agrees while guiding my hand up and down the length of him. I can feel every contour of his cock with my hand pressed this tightly around him and my breathing is increasing just from touching him.

"Lie back," he instructs, and I bite my lip and follow direction, scooting back on the bed as he crawls over me. His cock lies heavy on my stomach as he frames my face with his hands and kisses me. It's the longest kiss of my life, yet somehow the least awkward. My arms are wrapped around his neck and my nipples are brushing against his chest, causing all the nerve endings in my body to blaze. My heels are planted on the mattress while I raise my pelvis, trying to grind against him in any way that I can. But he doesn't hurry in the least.

His hands slide down from my face to explore while his lips cover every inch of my jaw and then make a slow descent down my neck until his tongue is running along my collarbone and I'm short of breath.

"You're really good at the kissing, Boyd," I manage to eke out.

"Glad to hear it." He continues tasting me everywhere he can reach.

"Yeah. Not slobbery at all."

"Thanks," he murmurs before taking a nipple between his lips and then nipping it with his teeth, the action causing a direct reaction straight into my core. I'm wetter than I've ever been in my life. He plays with my breasts for a long time, his hands never further than my waist when I'm dying for them to be moving south. His erection is heavy and warm against my shorts, so I move my hand down to stroke him. I'm rewarded with a grunt, so I squeeze him a little tighter and run my thumb around the crown. I don't know how he has the control to move this slowly and I'm not sure if I'm impressed or annoyed. Then his lips are journeying down my stomach as his fingers slide my pajama shorts and panties slowly down my thighs and finally over my ankles to the floor. When he keeps going I'm very glad I let Everly talk me into a regular waxing schedule.

I let my high-school boyfriend go down on me and it was okay, but mostly awkward for him and embarrassing for me so I never gave either guy I slept with in college the chance to attempt it. I have a momentary thought of pushing him away, but Boyd's not really asking and his confidence is a huge turn-on. Plus I'm curious. He's been really attentive with those lips so far.

When he uses his thumbs to spread me apart and runs his tongue up my center, my back bows and my thighs snap around his head. He chuckles, low and raspy, before sucking my clit between his lips as I loosen my grip on his head. Oh, holy hell. This is better than anything in the history of ever. Better than everything all added up.

"You taste even better than I thought you would," he murmurs from between my legs and I groan in response.

I'm dripping wet. Like, I suspect I'd be actually dripping if he wasn't consuming me like a starving man. I can't be any more vulnerable or exposed to him than in this moment and it gives me pause for a second but I'm in this now, with him and I'm going to enjoy tonight as long as it lasts. He's obviously into what he's doing so there's no need for me to feel insecure about it.

He slides a finger inside and I tighten around him, my body unused to the intrusion. He slides his finger out and in again as my muscles relax and allow him deeper without resistance. Two of his fingers are a stretch and he swears as I squirm, but it feels good. Pressure builds low in my core and explodes when he sucks my clit back between his lips and pumps into me with his fingers.

My hands fist into the bedspread as the orgasm tears through me. I've never come like that before. I'm not even sure I *have* come before if that's what it's supposed to feel like. "Boyd," I pant, still catching my breath.

He moves up my torso and nuzzles my neck as he speaks.

"Was that better than okay?" he asks, clearly remembering that I'd once indicated to him that my experience with sex was classified as okay.

"Yeah," I agree, my body still humming. "Definitely surpassed okay."

"Better than *Sex for Dummies*?"

"Maybe." A smile tugs at my lips.

"Maybe?" he questions, angling my chin towards him, his brow lifted in challenge. Have I mentioned how much I like his eyelashes?

"I don't know if I can leave you a review yet. We haven't finished."

"Ah." He nods. "So we should finish?"

"I'm definitely interested in finishing." I nod quickly. "I hate to review something I haven't finished."

He grins and shoves back on his arms then stands. Wait. Where is he going? I prop myself up on my elbows and watch him walk naked over to his suitcase. He has a nice ass too. I make a mental note to touch it while I have the chance. He turns back to the bed with a strip of condoms in his hand and that sobers me right out of my sexual stupor. Because I forgot about protection altogether. In all my psyching myself out over this encounter I never once thought about protecting myself physically.

"I totally forgot," I blurt out, eyeing the condoms.

"Don't worry, safety girl, I remembered." He tears one of the strip and tosses the rest aside. "I won't knock you up and trap you."

"Why would you want to trap *me*? That's not even

logical."

"It is from where I'm standing," he mutters as he tears the wrapper with his teeth and strokes himself, then straddles me on his knees and hands me the condom.

"Oh, I don't do that." I shake my head.

"You're open to anal but rolling a condom on is outside of your comfort zone?" he deadpans.

"Shut up. And I already told you anal was off the table once I got a look at your dick."

He pinches the end of the condom and places it against the head of his penis then takes my hand and moves it in place. I roll it over the length of him, alternating between watching what I'm doing and looking into his eyes. His never leave mine.

"Do you want me to do anything else?" I ask, but my voice is soft.

"Like what?" His lips curve into a small smile as he pushes me back against the bed and lies over me, bracing himself on his elbows.

"I don't know." I'm definitely whispering now and I shake my head a little. "I was worried you'd want me to do some weird thing."

"A weird thing?"

"Never mind. This is good. I like this." I run my hands up his biceps and dig the pads of my fingertips in a little, testing the feel of him.

He nudges my legs apart with his knee and settles between them and my heart rate skyrockets.

"It's been a while for me," I admit.

He nods and dips down to kiss me while sliding an arm under one of my knees, pulling me wider open. Then he continues with the kissing until I want to feel him inside of me so bad I'm aching. I flex my hips towards him, trying to get what I want, but he's not one to be rushed, apparently, because he continues to take his time kissing and caressing and generally driving me crazy until I wonder if I could come just from that alone.

Finally he's there, right where I want him. The tip of his cock nudges my opening and I suck in a breath but push my hips up. He slowly eases inside. The feeling of stretching to accommodate him is a slight burn that makes me crave more in the most hedonistic way.

I tilt my hips to accommodate him and he continues his drive into me until he bottoms out, our stomachs pressed flat together. He lowers his elbows until his forehead touches mine and he's so deep inside of me it's bordering on uncomfortable, yet I like it. I reach up and cup his jaw in my palm and guide his lips to mine, but this time I nip at his bottom lip, pulling it with my teeth.

"You are the most alluring woman I've ever met," he says when I release his lip.

Alluring? Not awkward? That can't be right.

I remember that I wanted to touch his ass while I had the chance and slide my hands down his back to my goal, planting my heels on the bed by his hips as I do. He grunts when my hands find their target, but the sound is sexy as hell. Husky, throaty—a verbal confirmation that he likes my touch. I flatten my hands against his backside and caress and I'm pretty sure that his ass is the most perfectly sculpted and toned ass I'll ever get my hands on.

He takes my prodding as an invitation to move and draws back before sliding into me again. And again. He's braced above me on his hands, watching my face as he thrusts and I feel exposed. Not physically so much as emotionally, like he sees too much. I place my hands back on his biceps, the leverage better for holding on, and try my best not to look away.

SEVENTEEN
BOYD

I knew she was going to feel good, but fuck. I'm ruined for this girl. Her skin. Her scent. Her taste. The texture of her hair and the delicate flare of her hips. The tiny mole she has near her belly button. The noises she makes when I touch her. None of it contrived. Her breathing speeding up and the little cries she makes are all pure Chloe. The way her fingertips explore my body with genuine curiosity, as if she's not the most familiar with the male form, not that she's attempting to inflate my ego.

' This is hard for her. Intimacy. Not the physical exactly. She likes this. I think it was getting to this place that was hard for her. Her confidence is safe with me. I want to protect it, cultivate it. Watch her flourish.

Being inside of her makes me feel like a goddamned king. But it's humbling too. Connecting with her like this, having her take me inside of her. Knowing she's trusting me to make it good for her.

I thrust and her eyes widen and she sucks in a little gasp of air, her lips forming a tiny o. Her pussy clenches around me so tightly I'm not sure it isn't hurting her, but she's so fucking wet for me that I slide further into her against all logic. The fit is so snug there shouldn't be room for me to move. But I do. Keeping the pace long and deep, rubbing her clit with my thumb. Watching the way her eyelids flutter or rise, the way she angles her neck or dips her hips, telling me what she likes, what feels best.

I wish I could fuck her without the condom. I want my cock coated in her, not latex. She was so wet when I fucked her with my fingers it was all I could do not to bend her in half and slam into her. And the taste of her, fuck. She tastes a little bit like that strawberry Chapstick she favors.

She's sweet. And warm and wet and oh so fucking tight. And brave too. She could have refused to come to Colorado with me. I wouldn't have blamed her. But I knew she was just curious enough, intrigued enough, to play along.

"Boyd." Her eyes are on mine and her jaw drops on a gasp. "I'm gonna come."

She seems almost surprised, as if she wasn't expecting it to happen again. As if I'd stop without it happening again, with me buried inside of her. Like there's a chance in hell that I'd miss that.

Her legs tighten against my sides and her fingers dig into my arms as her back arches. But that's nothing compared to the feel of her muscles spasming and tightening around my cock. I still for a moment, buried inside of her, then thrust again before I feel almost numb and my brain shuts off as I tense over her and my own orgasm bursts out of me.

I roll us over so I don't crush her, still buried inside of her. She's flopped on top of me, her limbs complete jelly and her head resting in the crook of my neck.

I'm fucked.

Everything I know about this girl tells me that tomorrow she's going to retreat. Downplay what is happening here and likely avoid the hell out of me.

"Chloe," I whisper, stroking her arm. I'm going to

have to move her. Get up and dispose of the condom. Offer her a towel. But that can wait a minute or two.

"Hmm?" she answers.

"What *do* you call a moose that plays a musical instrument?"

I feel her smile against my neck. "A moose-ician."

***

I wake up before she does. Her head is on my chest and her leg is flung over mine. I could slide out from under her and get up, but I'm enjoying sleepy Chloe too much. Her breathing is soft and even and her hair is wild and disheveled from the night before.

I know the exact moment she wakes. Her breathing pauses and she stiffens slightly in my arms. I watch her eyes blink open and stare at me and I wait for her reaction.

"Hi," I offer.

"Hi," she responds. Then she blinks a couple of times and rolls off of me.

"Are you good?" I ask. What the fuck do I mean by good? I wanted to ask if she was okay, but thought she would take offence at the question so I replaced it with good. Not sure that's any better.

"Yeah." She sits up and turns her head to look at me. Her hair sways across her shoulders and she tosses a smile in my direction. "You get five stars," she says and then hops off the bed and calls out that she's taking a shower as she disappears into the bathroom.

Soon we're packed and walking through the lobby. I've already called the valet and the car should be waiting by the time we make it outside. Chloe is falsely bright. It's subtle though. So subtle I imagine she pulls it off with most people. It's not real though. She's covering for her anxiety. She's not sure how to deal with the morning after. I'd try to talk to her about it, but I know it's going to be several days until she's ready. Until she's done battling whatever conversation she's having with herself in her head.

We're three steps away from the door when I hear my name being called out. It's my cousin Tommy. I'd consider ignoring him, but Chloe heard him too and has already stopped walking.

He catches up with us, his own suitcase in tow, and asks if we're headed to the airport. It's all downhill from there.

Chloe takes an instant liking to him. I'm not sure why because he's kind of a prick. Logically I know it's because she's grateful for the distraction—for the buffer between us after last night. But it doesn't make it any less irritating. They chat the entire way back to the regional airport in Gypsum and then the inevitable happens: Tommy skips his commercial flight in favor of taking the private jet back to Philadelphia with us.

"You don't mind, do you?" he asks. I mind. This guy has been a pain in my ass since childhood.

An hour later we're airborne and Tommy has installed himself in front of us in one of the swivel chairs turned backwards so he can spend the flight talking to Chloe. Fucker.

"Do you have anything else to do besides flirt with my girlfriend?" I ask him.

"Oh, stop," Chloe sighs in my direction then turns her attention to Tommy. "We met two weeks ago," she tells him, curving her thumb in my direction. "I'm just doing him a favor."

"Right on," Tommy says. Because he's the kind of guy

who still says 'right on.' Then he asks Chloe if she's a hooker.

I want to yell that she's mine and let him know he's treading on dangerous ground with me, but I know it would scare the shit out of Chloe. Not the yelling, but the claiming.

She laughs. "You think I could pass as a hooker?" she asks Tommy, seemingly not offended in the slightest. "You really think that someone would pay me for sex?"

"I'd pay you for sex," he responds.

I'm going to kill this fucker.

"No, not a hooker, but thank you." She smiles and leans back in her seat.

Who the hell says thank you when accused of being a hooker?

"Boyd brought me because he didn't want his mom trying to set him up," she adds.

"Who, Aunt Maureen? Nah, she knows Boyd's gay," Tommy replies and then laughs at his own joke.

"Yeah, no, he's not gay," Chloe replies with an earnest smile and a pat to my thigh. Tommy loses interest after that so I manage to pass the rest of the flight without wanting to kill him.

That lasts until we land and he asks for a ride into the city with us. And then he points out that he only lives a block from me so I can't even finagle dropping him off first. Asshole. Fake girlfriend cock-blocking asshole. So we drop Chloe off and I remind Tommy that I'm the one who bailed his dumb ass out when he got arrested for public intoxication on the Jersey Shore in college. Twice. And I'm the one who bought him condoms in high school. And also the one who covered for him when he broke Aunt Hilda's window with a baseball when we were kids. Let's just say I have a very long list.

In any case, Chloe's at home and I'm not with her. Which sucks. But this day likely wasn't going to end any differently, Tommy or no Tommy. She needs her space, time to think. Time to decide she wants to see me again without me pressuring her.

I can wait.

For now.

Eighteen
Chloe

It's Saturday. And I need a favor.

I make one last attempt to maneuver the bookcase into my car and then admit defeat and lean against the side of my Corolla while I think. He said he owed me a favor, right? That's what he said. So what would it hurt to ask? I could just text him and see if he responds. If he doesn't, no biggie. I know Sophie and Luke own an SUV. But Christine is three weeks old, I don't want to bother them.

I tap my foot on the lawn and try to summon up the courage to send a text. I am so stupid. It's a text. To a guy I slept with. It's not like he's a complete stranger. And it's not that big of a favor. But I hate asking for help. And what if he says no? I'll feel stupid and I hate feeling stupid.

Chloe: Are you busy?

Boyd: No.

Chloe: I need help moving something.

Chloe: If you're not busy.

Chloe: If you don't mind.

Boyd: I'll be right there.

Chloe: I'm not at home. It won't fit in my car. It's not a big deal. I can figure it out.

Boyd: Just give me the address, Chloe.

Chloe: One second.

I run back up the driveway and ask the lady what her house address is and then text it to Boyd. He texts back that he's on his way. So that was painless, I think. It's going to take him fifteen or twenty minutes to get here, so I leave the bookcase leaning against my car and walk to the house next door. I find a super-cool old frame and a mixing bowl that I'm pretty sure is older than me, but the vintage pattern on it makes me happy and I need one. Plus, it's only two dollars. I'm dropping them in my car when Boyd pulls up. I wave at him and he pulls in front of my car and parks, then gets out and walks back to me. He's in jeans and one of the raglan tees he picked up when we were in New York a couple of weekends ago. It fits him perfectly and reminds me that I know exactly what his chest looks like without the shirt. I feel myself flush and quickly try to think about something else.

"Thanks for coming," I offer while not looking at his chest.

"Chloe, this is a garage sale," he states unnecessarily while glancing up and down the street and then back to me.

"Did you want to look around before we load up the

bookshelf?" I ask him, pointing at the bookshelf that was just a couple inches too big to squeeze into my car.

"No." He laughs. "No, I'm good. Thanks." He looks me over and then reaches and wipes something off my cheek. "Eyelash," he tells me.

I feel anxious, wondering if he's laughing at my garage-sale shopping. "It's fun," I ramble off and cross my arms.

He looks momentarily confused then nods. "Sure. So are you done? Should I load this?" He pats the bookcase with his hand.

"Yeah, I'm ready. Thanks for the favor."

He gives me another quick glance before picking up the bookcase and walking it over to his SUV. Then we both get in our cars and I follow him back to my apartment.

Once inside he places it in the spot I indicate. "It's nice," he comments as he steps back and surveys it in my place. "Now what?"

Now what what?

"That was it. Thank you," I offer, a little confused.

"Lunch," he responds.

"Lunch? Um, well, I have laundry and stuff to do."

He pins me with an predatory glance and walks closer. I take a step back. Then another until I'm backed up against the wall. He leans down and I think he's going to kiss me but then he's tucking a strand of hair behind my ear and whispering.

"I'll do your laundry."

It takes me a minute because the tone he said it in was sexual rather than domestic. My mind has to catch up with the words and the fact that he just offered to do my laundry, not bend me over the kitchen table. And then I laugh. I give his chest a shove and laugh so hard I snort a little.

"What was that? A pickup line you use on beleaguered housewives? 'I'll do your laundry.'" Another giggle-snort escapes and I slap a hand over my mouth before adding, "I can't even."

Boyd just winks at me and then walks over to my bathroom, coming out with an armload of towels before crossing over to the closet where he finds my hamper and adds the towels before picking up the entire thing and heading for my front door.

"Hey!" I object.

"Do you have a washer and dryer in this place?" He pauses by my front door and glances around. "I didn't think so. Let's go." And he opens the door and walks out.

What. The. Hell?

"Boyd!" I chase him into the hallway. He's already two doors down by the time I catch up. "You can't just steal my laundry. It's weird. And kinda creepy."

"I think the words you're looking for are, 'Thank you.' I'm doing you a favor. You can use the washer and dryer at my place."

"Um…" I stall.

"You're welcome. Grab your purse."

The thing is, it's hard to say no to him. He's got this way of looking at me that makes me agreeable. He looks at me like he really sees *me*, which is thrilling, yet totally terrifying all at the same. So I follow him to his car and I get in.

It's not far to his place—less than two miles—but it's Center City, Philadelphia, so we sit in some traffic. He pulls into a covered parking spot that appears to be assigned to him and parks, then we head in. The building is very modern and urban and the interior hallways have an almost hotel-like feel. But then we step inside his unit and I realize it's a loft. A show-stopping, jaw-dropping loft. Hardwood floors play off the concrete ceiling and exposed ductwork. The walls are a mix of drywall and cement to break up the space with perfectly placed artwork and a wide screen television mounted to the wall. There's a dining room table that would easily seat six but looks like it's never used and a kitchen that's the perfect blend between modern and warm with stools around an enormous island that I imagine is used all the time. An industrial metal staircase leads up to what I assume is a bedroom loft, while floor-to-ceiling windows line the opposite wall.

Whoever decorated this place would twitch over my own second-hand decorating style, but I don't hate it. Quite the opposite. It's very inviting. I don't make any play at being polite, instead I walk around and investigate.

"What do you think?" Boyd asks when I turn back to him.

"When I was a kid I had this book about a mom bear and a dad bear and their twelve baby bears. And all the baby bears each had their own tree trunk—except the youngest. He was too little to have his own tree trunk, so he was still with Mom and Dad. Anyway, the other eleven baby bears each had a tree trunk and each one was different. Decorated to match their personalities. I was kinda obsessed with it."

"So you're saying you like my place?"

I laugh. "Yes. It suits you."

"Laundry is upstairs," he says. "Follow me." And then he jogs up the stairs while I trail behind him. I was correct in assuming there was a loft bedroom at the top of the stairs. The half wall is solid, offering privacy from below. But from the top, you can still experience the stunning windows and views. I'm eyeing the bedroom layout—and his bed—when I realize Boyd already has the water running into the washer in a laundry room attached to the bedroom and is dropping my towels into the machine.

"Hey!" I enter the laundry room and tug at the clothes basket. "You can't actually do my laundry."

"Yes, I can," he replies, straight-faced. "Who do you think does mine?"

"No. I mean, I'm sure you're capable but you're not touching my underwear and stuff."

"I've been inside of you. I don't think touching your underwear is encroaching on your privacy."

And just like that, things are weird. I blush. I actually feel my face turn red. I glance into the washer and watch the water pour in and wonder if this weirdness is all me or if he felt it too, but I don't want to look at his face to find out.

"Chloe." He says my name softly, but I can still hear it over the rushing water. He says it carefully, his tone easy, and I lift my eyes to meet his. "This doesn't have to be weird."

Okay. So he felt it too. I exhale and nod.

"No?"

"No. Besides, these are just the towels." Then he leans over me to reach the detergent. I stop breathing for a second when his body presses against mine. The memories of last weekend flash though my mind and I feel tingly all over. A moment later he's stepped back, detergent bottle in hand, and I exhale and watch as he measures the liquid and dumps it into the machine then snaps the lid closed.

I just stand there and stare at him, not moving. He cocks an eyebrow and then places his hands on my shoulders and turns me around.

"Now lunch," he says.

"Now lunch," I agree. I pause at the top of the stairs and wave at the windows. "This must be amazing at night," I say and then cringe. Holy cow, did that sound like I was inviting myself to stay? "I mean, I can imagine that it does," I add and then shake my head and jog down the steps. "Hey, do you know why Adele crossed the road?"

"Nope."

"To say hello from the other side."

We reach the bottom of the steps and I turn to look at him. He's staring back at me with a dubious expression. "Come on, that one was good."

"It was something," he agrees. "What do you want for lunch?"

"I don't know." I shrug. "A sandwich?"

"Then I've got just the place."

***

We leave his place and head east on South Street to 5th then cut across Bainbridge to 4th Street. He offered to drive, but I opted for walking. It'll be only too soon before the weather turns and makes walking miserable. It's still nice for now, might as well take advantage of it.

"Thanks for helping me get the bookcase home," I offer as we walk. I'm not sure why we're still together. Why he wanted to have lunch, offered to let me do his laundry at his place.

"No problem. Gotta work off those favors I owe you, right?"

Favors? "How many favors do you owe me?"

"Two."

"Two?"

"Yeah. It was three, but I paid one off with the bookcase. So two."

"When did we decide you owed me three favors?" This guy totally does math like a government employee.

"Didn't we?" He looks totally nonplussed with his bad accounting of favors. "We're here."

"The Famous 4th Street Delicatessen," I read from the sign as Boyd holds the door. "I've never been here."

"What? Chloe." He shakes his head and makes a tsk sound. "What kind of a Philadelphian are you?"

"Well, I'm from Connecticut, so…"

"Weak excuse, Chloe. Weak."

We get a table and Boyd orders two cream sodas. The place has a retro old-fashioned feel that makes it feel like it's been there forever, which a glance at the menu tells me it just about has. 'Since 1923' is proudly printed on the front. I read through the menu and when the waitress comes we both place the same order—a turkey sandwich.

Then I stare at him for a while trying to determine what he wants.

And if I want to give it to him.

And then I start to panic a little. What if he wants to have an awkward conversation? Like more awkward than me? Or ask me about my sexual history? Or if I cheated on my third-grade spelling test in Mrs. Kallam's class?

Okay, I admit that last one is a little specific and not likely to come up. But I'm still a little ashamed of myself for doing it.

"Would you rather eat stale pretzels or stale Cheetos?"

"What?" I look at him, not sure I heard him correctly. He tilts his head in a nod, like, 'you heard me correctly,' but repeats the question.

"Um, stale pretzels, I guess."

"Go a week without the internet or a week without

coffee?"

Oh, we're playing the 'would you rather' game. "Internet." I smile. "I think. Wait maybe the coffee? No, the internet."

"Play Quidditch or use the invisibility cloak for a day?"

"You did not just Harry Potter me."

"I did."

"Well, I'm not sure that's even answerable." I shake my head and groan a little. "Who wouldn't want to play Quidditch? But the invisibility cloak, wow." I sigh, a dreamy expression on my face.

Boyd just stares as if he's not moving on until I answer.

"Quidditch." I finally relent.

"Why?"

"It looks like fun. Plus the invisibility cloak is basically spying, right? And I don't really need to spy on anyone so it would be a waste."

"No point in being wasteful," he agrees.

"Plus I've always had a sneaking suspicion that I'd be really good at Quidditch." And I can't help it. This tidbit comes out a little smugly. Boyd lasts two seconds before laughing at me.

When the food arrives my mouth drops.

"Boyd, this is enough food to feed four people. Why didn't we split one sandwich?"

"We might need the leftovers. Laundry is serious business."

He says laundry, but I'm not sure he's talking about laundry. I pull half the turkey off the bread so that it will fit in my mouth and take a bite, but my eyes drift sadly towards the bakery case we passed on the way in.

"You can still get dessert if you don't finish your

sandwich, Chloe."

"That's not what I was thinking about," I object.

"Yes, it was."

He's right, of course.

"How do you do that?"

"Read your mind?"

"I don't think you can read my mind." I tilt my head and look at him skeptically. We wouldn't have made it out of his apartment if he'd been reading my mind.

He just raises one brow and smiles in that way that he does. It makes my heart race and my nerves flare. Time to change the subject.

"Too bad you don't have a cat."

"A cat? Why?" He nabs a fry and stuffs it in his mouth in one bite.

"All this leftover turkey. Plus those windows at your place. A cat would love those windows."

"What would I call it?"

"The cat?"

"Yeah."

"Snoogledoralicious," I offer.

"That's pretty specific."

"Yeah." I nod and take a fry for myself. "But your cat would be special. You wouldn't want to call him something ordinary like Tom. Everyone has a cat named Tom."

"Of course they do," he agrees with a single nod.

We finish eating, both of us with half a sandwich packed to go—and a black and white cookie for me—and start the walk back to Boyd's.

"Tell me a crime story."

"A crime story? Is that like a fairy tale for girls obsessed with crime shows?"

"Exactly!" I bounce a little with excitement and swing

the bag with our leftovers. "You get me!"

"That I do," he agrees. "Okay, let me think of one that's not classified," he says and, well, obviously that turns me on. Plus he's got scruff today. I'm not sure I've seen him unshaven. It's a good look for him. Clean shaven is a good look too. Oh, hell, I imagine he'd be hard pressed to look bad. And I can't help but check out how well his jeans fit when we pause to cross the street at the corner of South and 5th. And then I wonder if we're going to have sex again because last weekend was... I want to do that again. I'd half given up believing that sex was more than an awkward exchange that resulted in feeling sorta good. But Boyd made me a believer that there might be something I'm missing out on. I wonder what that scruff would feel like on my skin and if I'm the only one of us thinking about all this stuff.

"Chloe." He's a couple of steps ahead of me and he's turned back, his expression questioning. "The light is green," he says.

Okay. I might be the only one of us thinking dirty thoughts in the middle of South Street. Also, pretty sure he just caught me looking at his ass.

NINETEEN
BOYD

We get back to my place and head upstairs to toss her towels in the dryer and start a new load with her clothing. I wonder how long it will take her to bolt. I figure I have until her clothing dries before she tells me she needs to leave.

I stand back while she drops her clothing into the washer, letting her handle her garments since that seemed to bother her. Besides, this gives me the chance to stare. And I like looking at Chloe. Her hair falls around her face as she reaches into the basket to pull things out and then sways against her back as she stands. I wonder if I can have sex with her today without disturbing the friendship between us. Because I'd really like to have sex with her again. And I have no interest in being just her friend.

But this is Chloe.

I can't read her mind, but I can read her body perfectly. The subtle walls she throws up. The way her pulse increases over the simplest social interaction between us. The way her hand trembles when she rips up a sweetener packet. Or how she blinks then looks ninety degrees to the left when she's second-guessing herself. She blows out the tiniest puff of a breath then sucks her bottom lip into her mouth when she's thinking about talking herself out of something and she's a little bit snarky when she's intimidated.

So I can be patient.

She's clearly got social anxiety and that will cause her to go great lengths to avoid any situation that makes her uncomfortable.

I make her uncomfortable.

But she likes me.

I know that too from reading her. She lights up when she sees me. She wets her lips when I get close to her and her pupils dilate. She shifts her body weight to one hip and leans towards me the tiniest fraction of an inch. And she keeps agreeing to see me. I know if she wasn't interested she'd tell me to fuck off.

And I like her. She makes me laugh. The way she tells those ridiculous jokes when she's nervous and how crime shows fascinate her. I love the way she eyes me with skepticism while she thinks about whether she's going to give in to whatever I throw at her.

So I'll be patient with her. Even if it kills me.

Sex isn't her hangup. I didn't fool myself into thinking if I got her into bed last weekend that all of her anxieties would just cease. I know it doesn't work like that. So we'll face her anxiety one date at a time—even if she doesn't know they're dates. The more time I can spend with her the more of a routine we can build. And the more I can boost her confidence for doing things that are difficult for her. But I've got to be strategic. If I push for too much too soon she's going to shut down and not let me in. She'll focus too much on panicking instead of on us.

I wanted to call her all week. Text her, have dinner. Anything. If she was any other girl it would have been a dick move *not* to have called her. But I suspected that Chloe needed me not to call. Needed the time to think and decide in her own way that she wanted to see me again without me pressuring her.

She finishes loading her clothing and I add the detergent and close the lid then look at her. Her eyes widen and her breath hitches. I could take her on top of the washing machine right now. I'd like to take her on top of the washing machine right now. But first, we need another moment together that's not about sex.

"*Criminal Minds* marathon on all day," I tell her.

"What?" She blinks.

"Come on." I turn and walk out of the laundry room and head for the stairs. "What do you want to drink?"

"Um, what do you have?" she asks. I can hear her behind me on the stairs, her pace slow.

I grab the TV remote on the way to the kitchen and flick the TV on then scroll through to the channel running the marathon. Tossing the remote on the kitchen island, I open the fridge and start calling out options to Chloe as she wanders over to the sofa then pauses and walks to the windows to check out my view instead.

I set our drinks on the coffee table and then join her at the window.

"You should see it at night," I tell her.

"Um, yeah," she says as noncommittally as I expected her to and strolls over to the couch. "This was a good episode," she says and takes a seat.

So we watch *Criminal Minds* and toss a list of 'would you rather' questions at each other until the washer stops. Then I follow her upstairs to supervise while she folds her towels and transfers her wet clothing from the washer to the dryer. I stand in the doorway watching her and yes, it occurs to me how whipped I am for this girl that watching her fold towels does it for me.

She finishes with the exception of a couple of lacy bras clutched in her hand.

"These, um, don't go in the dryer," she says while avoiding my eyes.

"Relax, I've seen a bra before, Chloe. Don't worry, I won't lose my shit." I step into the laundry room and reach over her to grab a hanger for her. She drapes the straps over the neck of the hanger and then reaches to get the hanger to the rod. But it's a stretch for her. And did I mention that she's wearing another pair of those clingy fucking leggings?

This pair is black but they don't leave any more to my imagination than any of the previous pairs I've seen her in did. Her shirt rides up when she stretches, raising the hemline to her waist and exposing a small band of skin. It also gives me a direct view of the perfect soft curve of her ass.

She pops onto her toes to give herself that extra inch of reach and I slide my hands around her waist and turn her, then lift her onto the dryer. She wraps her legs around me and things escalate pretty quickly from there. In fact, as I slide my hand under her shirt and cup her tit, I'm confident I know exactly how this ends. But then Chloe surprises me.

"Wait," she says, breaking her lips from mine and placing a palm against my chest, pushing me back a few inches.

Wait? Dammit, I pushed this too soon. She looks momentarily dazed, her skin flushed, pupils dilated and hair messed.

"Can I," she starts and stops, her tongue darting out to wet her lips and her eyes glancing downward. "I want to try something before you distract me."

She wants to try something? I move my hands to either side of her on the dryer, caging her in. "What did you want to try, Chloe?" Please say it's your lips, wrapped around my dick.

Her fingers grasp my belt and she tugs at the buckle then flicks her eyes to mine before quickly glancing away again.

"I wanted to give you a blow job."

Well, my day is made.

I take over for her, swiftly unbuckling my belt. "Great. I'd like you to try that too," I respond.

"I'm, um, I'm not sure that I'm that great at it though. Like I'm not terrible." She pauses. "I don't think. Average probably." She bites her lip. "Maybe the lower end of average?"

Fucking hell. Why does the idea of Chloe fumbling her way through this make my dick swell?

She glances up, making eye contact, her green eyes no longer dazed but curious. "I thought you could give me some pointers?"

She wants me to teach her how to give a better head? My balls are already so heavy I don't know how long this lesson is going to last. But I'm happy to find out.

I pull her off the dryer, wrapping her legs around me and walking with her to the bedroom, placing her on her feet at the foot of the bed.

"Do you want to sit on the bed or kneel on the floor?"

She tilts her head back to meet my gaze. "What's hotter for you?" she asks.

"Get on your knees."

She does. Instantly sinking to the floor as her tongue sweeps her bottom lip.

"You start," I tell her. "We'll take it from there."

My pants hit the floor and I groan as she wraps a hand around the base of my cock. Her touch is soft and she uses her grip to guide the tip to her mouth, wrapping her lips around me, her tongue flat on the underside of my dick.

Perfect.

I don't know what Chloe is worried about. It's pretty hard to fuck this up. It's pretty much un-fuckup-able.

She swirls her tongue around the tip of my cock as I wrap my hands into her hair, her eyes flicking up in question. I grunt instructions to continue and she bobs her head up and down, working the rest of me with her fist. Her eyes remain on mine and this could not be any better. I've had women give head like a porn star, but they weren't Chloe. Sitting on her knees with her lips stretched around me while looking me straight in the eye.

But then she stops, sits back on her heels and looks at me from beneath her lashes. "Tell me what else to do," she says. "Tell me how to make it better for you."

"It's perfect, Chloe."

But she shakes her head no before I'm finished speaking. "Tell me. Just one thing," she adds when I don't answer her quickly enough.

"Give me your hand," I tell her and she looks surprised for a moment but does. I wrap mine over hers and guide her to cup my balls, squeezing her hand gently. She catches on and takes over from there. Her hand is so fucking soft as she cups them, gently massaging as she takes me back into her mouth and wraps her other hand around my shaft again.

I'm not going to last.

Perfect 2.0.

And when I tell her I'm going to come and she sucks harder?

Best. Day. Ever.

I fall onto the bed after, white spots still impairing my vision while Chloe crawls onto the bed beside me and lies in the crook of my arm while my heart rate returns to normal.

"Five stars," I say, remembering what she said to me in Vail, and she smiles against my chest. And then I make sure that smile is replaced with a gasp and a lot of moans as I return the favor.

Gasps and moans and toe-curling and an 'Oh, my God, Boyd, I don't think I can come again,' later, I'm moments away from suggesting we move this into the shower for round three when she sits up.

"The dryer stopped."

And with that she's out of bed and putting her clothing back on.

"I should go," she says, as she stuffs her arms into the sleeve of her shirt. "I have lesson plan stuff." She slides it over her head and lifts an ankle to slip those ridiculous non-pants on over her foot. "And I need to dust." The other ankle goes through and then she's pulled the leggings to her waist and dashed into the laundry room. I get out of bed and pull my jeans back on sans underwear and follow her. She's not even folding her clothes, just stuffing them straight from the dryer to the basket. "I can walk. Or take a cab." She turns to see me standing in the doorway, her eyes on my naked chest. "Or walk," she repeats.

"I'll drive you," I tell her. "Let me get a shirt."

"A shirt would be good," I hear her say behind me and I can't help but grin, glad she can't see my face. This girl is a mess of conflicting emotions, but good things come to those who wait. And Chloe is a good thing. A forever kind of thing.

Twenty

Chloe

"You cannot be serious."

"I am."

"You need *another* favor?" It's two weeks after the Vail trip and a week since I saw him last—when I did laundry at his house. And other stuff. "Don't you still owe me two favors?"

"So I'll owe you three, which is a big deal. You could cash in three favors for one really big favor."

Yes. Yes, my mind does instantly detour into the gutter.

"I don't know," I mumble.

"Chloe. I'm not even making this up. I really need your help."

"What is it? I'm not getting on an airplane."

"Meet me at the book store down the street. At 18th and Walnut."

"The book store?" I ask, my voice dripping sarcasm. "Really, Boyd? Are you being serious right now or is this one of your weird come-on lines? 'Oh, Chloe, I'll do your laundry,'" I purr into the phone in a sexy voice. "'Chloe, I have an emergency at the book store. Hurry,'" I add in the same tone. "Please, Boyd," I finish, my voice back to snarky.

177

He laughs, his voice a throaty chuckle over the phone, and I can picture his smile as he does. I wonder if he shaved today or if he's sporting the day-old scruff look. "No, this is legitimate. Hurry up." Then he hangs up on me before I can object again.

What a weirdo.

But I put my shoes on all the same. And check my reflection in the bathroom mirror while I'm brushing my hair. And sure, I freshen my Chapstick and put on a little mascara. But I'd put on mascara for a run to Starbucks. It doesn't mean anything.

I exit my building and head down Walnut. The book store is all of three blocks away so I'll walk. I wonder what Boyd wants and why he is hanging out in a book store late on a Saturday afternoon. I am not having a quickie with him in the history section, if that's what he's thinking. Absolutely. Am not.

Less than fifteen minutes after he called I'm in the store. I don't see him anywhere and I could text him and ask where he is, but I'm sorta curious about what he's up to. So I'll poke around a bit first and see if I can't find him without alerting him that I'm here yet.

I almost miss him, because he's not alone. I finally find him at a table at the in-store Starbucks. And he's sitting with a boy who looks like he's about nine or ten and what appears to be homework spread across the table.

"Hi," I say and two sets of eyes flick up to meet mine.

"Yo, is this your girlfriend?" the kid asks, appraising me. "She's hot."

His girlfriend? Are we pretending again?

Boyd tilts his head at the kid and gives him a stern look. "Noah. We've been over this."

The kid sighs, as if the weight of the world is on him,

dramatically slumping and rolling his eyes before he sits up straight and looks me in the eyes. "Hello. I'm Noah. It's nice to meet you." He's wearing a Philadelphia Eagles hoodie and his dark hair is disheveled, as if he's been running his hands through it with no care for how it looks.

Then he stands and offers me his hand. I shake it as I reply, "Nice to meet you too, Noah. I'm Chloe."

"You're very pretty," he adds, then glances back at Boyd. "Better?"

"Better."

"So what's going on here?" I ask when Boyd is done playing Miss Manners with Noah.

"New math. That's what's going on here." Boyd indicates to an open textbook and papers spread across the table. "Something that schools refer to as Common Core but adults cannot comprehend."

"It's stupid!" Noah interjects. "I have a calculator on my phone. Why do I even need math?"

"Well," I start as I slide into a chair and join them, "it's important that you understand the basics, so that later you'll have the foundation that'll make it easier to learn more complicated math concepts."

"But why can't I just use the internet?" he asks me, expression sincere.

"Because math is about learning logic and critical thinking. Math teaches you life skills and quick thinking. It's not just about calculating a number that you could look up. It's about problem-solving." I pull his paper closer to me and take a look. "So, tell me where you're stuck."

It takes us about a half hour to work through Noah's math homework. He's a smart kid, and once it's explained to him in a way that he understands we zip through the assignment. Boyd stays the entire time, paying attention and telling Noah to focus a couple of times when he wants to give up. But I don't understand what their relationship to each other is, and I realize it wasn't offered when I arrived. When Noah starts to pack up his books my curiosity gets the best of me.

"So, Noah is your..." I direct the question at Boyd and trail off, expecting him to fill in the blank. But he doesn't. Noah beats him to it.

"He's my dad," he says, dropping pencils haphazardly into the bag.

"Noah," Boyd says, and I can't tell if his tone is a warning or a defeat.

"I don't know what kind of lies he's been telling you. But you seem like a nice lady to me, and you deserve to know the truth." Noah sighs and looks me straight in the face. "I'm his love child."

Um, what? He has a child? No way.

Boyd wraps his arm around Noah's head and slaps his palm over his mouth to shut him up. "Knock it off, Noah. And how do you even know what a love child is?" He ruffles Noah's hair with his other hand then releases him.

"I'm ten, not stupid," Noah responds, scrunching his eyebrows and giving Boyd a look. "He's my big," Noah says, looking back to me.

"Your big?" I repeat and look at Boyd. "You're a mentor?" I ask, guessing that Noah is referring to the Big Brothers, Big Sisters program. One of the kids in my class has a big and the teacher I student-taught under during college was also involved in the program. They match adult volunteers with children who have signed up looking for a role model. They commonly refer to the adults as bigs and the kids as littles, and the relationships can last a year or a lifetime. Usually it's a few hours a month spent helping the little with homework or taking them to do something fun.

"Yeah." Boyd nods. "And I got matched with this little punk," he says affectionately.

"There was a line for me," Noah responds. "You just got lucky."

"Well, I'm glad I could help. And it was really nice meeting you, Noah." I push my chair back and stand.

"Aren't you coming with us to the ghost thing?" Noah glances at me, seeming surprised that I'm leaving, then turns to Boyd. "Boyd, can Chloe come with? I like her," he pleads.

"Of course she can come," Boyd responds. "Unless she's afraid of ghosts. She might be too chicken." He looks at me as he says it, like a challenge. And Noah jumps right in and squawks at me.

"Where is it that you're going?" I laugh. "Ghost hunting?"

"It's a ghost tour!" Noah bursts out in excitement. "We're gonna see a bunch of haunted places."

I bite my lip and look between them. It's harmless, right? I mean, not the ghosts. Ghosts aren't real. But hanging out with Boyd and Noah. It's not a date. It's just... hanging out. Nothing to panic about. I'm good at hanging out. And Noah is here, and I'm good with kids.

"Sure, I'll go."

And that's how I end up spending most of the evening with Boyd. Again. And sleeping with him. Again. But it so wasn't a date. Because when I start to think that there's something happening between us I freak out. Second-guess myself. Wonder if he's going to call again or if I've said something stupid. I start running conversations through my mind over and over again until my heart races and I start to envision ways that this could end badly. Ways that will end up with me being hurt. Or Boyd being hurt. What if I hurt him? I don't want to hurt him. I don't want to hurt anyone.

Then I wonder if I'm crazy to even let my thoughts wander *there* in the first place. Boyd is freaking amazing. Hot. Wealthy. Incredible in bed. He volunteers with children, for crying out loud. He's practically perfect in every way. Like Mary Poppins. If Mary Poppins was an attractive thirty-two-year-old man with magic sex skills and an interest in me.

He cannot be interested in me. In what I want. Which is not casual. What we're doing right now—the sex and the hanging out—is fun. And I'm enjoying myself. Anyone would. But if we keep doing this I'm going to fall in love with him and then I'll want more. Or I'll freak out and need to breathe into a paper bag, hard to tell with me.

But what did he say about taking me to Vail instead of taking a *real* date? Something about real dates reading into things. Kinda like I'm doing right now.

Maybe there's nothing to read into.

So I'm going to stop.

Besides, it wasn't a date.

TWENTY-ONE
BOYD

"Hey, Boyd! Good to see you. Come on in." My sister beams at me from the doorway of her condo. Baby Christine is asleep in her arms. Or arm. Looks like Sophie's already mastered the one-armed baby carry because she's still got one hand on the door and the baby cradled in her opposite arm.

I step inside and we walk down to the kitchen where Sophie offers me coffee, then sets the baby in my arms while she makes it.

"You seem happy," I comment, while baby Christine blinks up at me while scrunching her nose up like she's about to cry. But she must decide I'm a passable temporary replacement for Sophie because her features relax and she waves her tiny fist in my general direction. I give her my finger to latch onto and she grips on with surprising strength for such a little person. Surprising to me at least.

"Yeah, I am." Sophie beams from across the room. She's got a new-mom glow about her and I suspect that Sophie's going to be one of those moms who embrace motherhood with gusto. I wonder what it would be like to grow up with one of those moms, the really good ones, and then I find myself wondering what Chloe would be like as a mom; it's not that hard to imagine. I've seen her with Sophie's baby and Everly's kid. And she was great yesterday with Noah. Not great—amazing. I know she's a teacher, but I've never gotten to *see* her teach before. She's one of the great ones. It's her element, for sure.

"She's such a good baby," Sophie continues. "She's making it really easy on me. And Luke always makes me feel like I'm doing everything right, which is reassuring. So yeah, things are great."

"I guess she's about a month old now, isn't she?" I calculate as Sophie sets our beverages down and sits next to me at the table.

"Yeah," she says. But her tone implies something else and the skin between her eyebrows wrinkles in the slightest way. "Almost a month," she amends in a rush. "In two days. She's twenty-eight days old now." Then she blows out a long breath and shakes her head before meeting my eyes. "I'm one of those moms, Boyd. I promised myself that I wasn't going to be. But I'm clearly on a path there. I'm that mom who's going to tell you her kid is forty-nine months old when all you wanted to hear is that she's four." She shakes her head again and rolls her eyes to the ceiling. "It's so embarrassing."

I laugh at her and she looks at me, chagrined. "I'm sure it's very exciting," I allow as I glance down at the baby. She blinks back at me then yawns and, yeah, it's fucking adorable.

"So how are things with you?" Sophie asks, her tone striving for nonchalant. "Are you seeing anyone?" She takes a sip of her drink and appraises me over the rim of her mug.

"Are you worried about my love life?" Deflect without lying. I raise my eyebrows and give her a look of confusion.

"What did you think of my friend Chloe?" she asks. "You met her at the hospital when I had Christine. Remember? With the long brownish-reddish hair? Really pretty?"

"Chloe." I nod. "Are you trying to set me up with your friend?" I raise an eyebrow in challenge.

"She's a really nice girl, Boyd. I think you two would totally hit it off."

"I don't think a set-up is necessary," I say as nonchalantly as possible while straightening the footie pajamas on Christine's toes. "But thanks."

Down the hall the front door opens and a moment later her husband Luke walks into the kitchen, clearly just back from the gym.

"Hey, babe," Sophie calls out to him as he grabs a bottle of water from the fridge and walks over to say hello. "Before I forget, Chloe called and wanted to know if you could attend career day with her class next month. I put it on your calendar."

"Sure," Luke agrees and bends over to kiss the top of Sophie's head.

"Why didn't she ask me to come to career day?" I wonder. But apparently it's out loud because they both turn to look at me, Sophie with confusion, Luke in assessment.

"Why would Chloe ask you to do her a favor, Boyd? She doesn't even know you," Sophie says, a little baffled and with complete reason. Because obviously I just insinuated I didn't know her and wasn't interested in getting to know her. All of two minutes ago. Luke unscrews the cap to the water bottle and watches, the hint of a smirk on his face as he silently lets me dig myself a hole.

"Uh. You know how little kids love the Feds. That's all."

"What grade is it that Chloe teaches again, Sophie? I forget," Luke comments before taking a sip of water. Now I'm sure he's fucking with me.

"Second," Sophie tells him then glances back at me. "Wait, did I tell you Chloe is a teacher?"

"You said career day with her class. What else would she be?" Yeah, I think I've crossed the line from deflecting into lying now.

"Oh, right. Okay," Sophie agrees. "Are you sure I can't introduce you again? I could have you both over and I wouldn't even tell her it's a set-up," she tells me, beaming with excitement over her plan. "Plus, she gets really nervous. So it'd be easier if she didn't know anyway. Or I could ask her to babysit and you could just happen to stop by," she says, waving her hands excitedly about her set-up ideas.

"I think you've been spending too much time with that scheming friend of yours."

"Everly?" Sophie asks, not missing a beat. "Please. If

185

Everly was conspiring this set-up you wouldn't even know it was happening. She'd probably get you both drunk and you'd wake up married in Vegas," she says, laughing. Then she stops. "Actually, I wouldn't put that past her. Nobody put that idea in her head."

"I'm gonna hop in the shower," Luke interrupts. I guess bro code is finally kicking in. "Boyd, the game is about to start. You gonna stay and watch?"

I nod. "Sounds good," I agree, but I'm a little bit distracted. Why didn't Chloe ask me to do career day at her school? She asked Sophie's husband but not me? Does she only think of me as some kind of friend with benefits? Maybe all she's interested in with me is sex?

Or maybe she just doesn't want to take that leap into real. At least not with me. I remind myself that she's only twenty-two and wonder if I'm expecting too much from her. I sure as hell didn't want to be tied down to anyone when I was twenty-two.

I'll wait, if I have to. But I need some confirmation from her that she wants what I want.

I want Chloe tied to me.

TWENTY-TWO
BOYD

I text her from the lobby and tell her I'm on my way up. Having a badge is a really convenient way to get past building security. Not that this place has much.

She's standing in the open doorway of her apartment when I get off the elevator, hand on her hip with her head cocked to the side in question. "I brought donuts," I offer by way of explanation for showing up unannounced.

"Did you need a favor or something?" she asks, taking the box from my hands and setting it on the tiny round dining table just inside the door of her apartment. Not a promising start, but she does allow me to follow her inside.

"I just brought you a favor," I comment then eye her. "Do you own *any* pants?" She's wearing another pair of those godforsaken leggings.

"What are you talking about? I'm wearing pants right now. And how does this count as a favor when I didn't ask for it? It shouldn't count towards my favor tally if I didn't make the official request." She pops open the donut box and peeks inside. "You're like the worst genie ever."

"I know. But your favors are piling up. I gotta work them off. And those aren't pants."

"Leggings are pants. They're very popular."

"What the hell is even on them?" I step closer and eye her ass, focusing on the print. Purely for research purposes. "Are those black cats?"

"They're my seasonal leggings!" she retorts and selects a donut as I walk past her into the tiny aisle of a kitchen and pour myself a cup of coffee.

"Oh. Did you want something to drink? Let me get that for you," she says sarcastically before biting into a donut.

I ignore her tone. "No, no. I've got it, thank you." I take the mug and pass by her, taking a seat on her couch. She's arranged some books on the shelves along with a couple of small knick knacks. "Bookshelf looks good."

She looks at me sitting on her sofa, confusion crossing her face. "Okay, you're staying," she says, but I think it's more to herself than to me. "Do you want a donut?"

"No, thanks."

"Okay." She exhales and walks closer to me then realizes she either needs to sit next to me on a two-person sofa or sit on her bed. She finds a third option and sits on the trunk coffee table between us instead, one leg on the floor and one bent in front of her on the trunk. "So," she says, her eyes running over me. They pause on my lips and then she takes another bite of the donut in her hand.

"So," I reply back.

"Are you here to do my laundry?" she asks.

I laugh. "No, but we can bring it and do it after."

"After what?" she asks, eyeing me with interest, her guard up.

"There's a flea market today over in Society Hill. I thought we could go."

Her eyes widen the tiniest bit and her foot bounces a

couple of times against the hardwood floor.

"A flea market?" she questions.

"Just like a garage sale. But outside. In a park."

"I, um," she stammers. "I know what a flea market is."

I know she knows what a flea market is. And I know she's waiting for me to tell her this is a favor. That I have a sudden need to find an ugly old painting or a vintage magic eight-ball and that I need her to help me do it. But I don't. Because I need her to meet me on this. I need her to start thinking about us as more than whatever it is she does. So I remain silent and keep my eyes steady on her. And wait.

"Um, yeah. Okay," she agrees.

"Okay," I say casually.

"I'll grab my stuff," she says, rising. "And don't think I'm not bringing my laundry."

***

We stop at my place to drop my car and start a load of her laundry then walk to the flea market. It's every bit as hellish as one would expect. The flea market, not the walk. The walk is great. The flea market is a giant outdoor garage sale. Filled with used junk. Other people's used junk.

Or, from Chloe's viewpoint: treasures.

Okay.

But Chloe loves it, and I love her so I'm willing to do what it takes to spend the day with her.

Old black-and-white pictures of other people's relatives. Used hats. A vintage mail box, rotary phones. One guy is selling fresh fruit and vegetables, which makes no sense to me at all, but Chloe stops and buys a couple of apples.

A short while later she pauses in front of a box of old house numbers. It's on the pavement in a cardboard box that looks ready to give out from the weight of the items inside of it, but that doesn't deter Chloe from stooping down and digging through, pulling out a two and setting it on the brick sidewalk beside her before digging back in.

This makes less sense than the fresh green beans located next to the recycled tires turned into planters we passed ten tables ago, but I'm game.

"What are we looking for?" I ask, squatting down next to her. She pulls out a zero and places it next to the two. They're completely mismatched. Different fonts, sizes, materials and age. But she seems happy with her search.

"A four," she replies. The numbers in the box rattle as she rummages until they fall silent as she plucks out a four in victory. "There." She places it on the pavers in front of the two and the zero.

"A four, a two and a zero," I comment. "Are you moving?"

"No!" She laughs as she says it, her head turning in my direction, her hair falling in a curtain around her. "Like the four-twenty highway shirt I almost bought in Vail. I'm going to hang these on the wall over my bookcase. It'll remind me of that day."

Then she smiles. And fuck, that does things to me.

"Great idea. I'll get a set too," I tell her. "Help me find three more."

So that's how we end up with an entire box of used house numbers spread around on the ground while we inspect the available options of fours, twos and zeros until we both have the mismatched set we like best. And fine, I'm starting to see the appeal of other people's used shit. Because this is fun. Chloe is fun.

Everything with Chloe is more fun. Donuts and

shopping and traveling on the candy plane—it's all better when she's around. Errand-running and laundry and hours spent at a flea market. I'll take it. Because I know that every day I spend with Chloe is the best day of my life.

We poke around the market for another couple of hours. I'm happy to find someone selling coffee. Chloe is happy to find enough old wooden toy blocks to spell out Christine. She insists my sister will love them for the baby's vintage-chic nursery. I don't have a fucking clue, but I nod and agree anyway. We walk back towards my place on Pine Street, which turns out to be antique row in Center City, Philadelphia. Two blocks of shops filled with a variety of kitsch, vintage and antique stores. Which by my way of thinking is a bunch of garage sales located inside of storefronts, but I'll admit once we step inside a few they have some pretty cool stuff. I even manage to find a really cool original sketch of the hospital Sophie's husband works at. I get it for him even though he's an annoying fuck. He does love my sister.

When we make it back to my place Chloe runs upstairs to move her laundry into the dryer and I grab my tool box and follow her up.

That's not a euphemism. I have an actual tool box. I want to hang the numbers we got today over my dresser so I'll see them every morning when I wake up.

Jesus fuck.

Why don't I just beg her to marry me and get it over with?

Once Chloe finishes with her laundry she watches me affix the numbers to my wall, helping me decide on the placement.

Then everything goes to shit.

"Do you want to order something in for dinner or go

out?" I ask her.

She's sitting on the end of my bed watching me pack up the toolbox. I snap the latches closed and glance at her.

"What are we doing, Boyd?" She waves her hands by her face, her fingers spread wide like little explosions. "I mean seriously. What are we doing?" She grabs a strand of her hair and starts twirling it around her finger, her movements rough and slightly panicky. Her legs are crossed and the foot touching the floor starts to bounce.

Shit. All I mentioned is dinner. I haven't even mentioned the five-year plan for a house in the suburbs. Which I shouldn't be thinking about, but I do. Because this girl is a fucking whirlwind to my common sense. She makes me think about forever with her when I haven't even nailed her down to the next date.

"We should break up," she says. "I'm a disaster. I'll fuck everything up. I always fuck it up." Her voice is distressed and she looks like she's on her way to hyperventilating. "And you'll leave. Everyone leaves. And I don't know what I'm doing."

"You can't break up with me. We're not dating," I reply calmly and cross over to her, taking her hand so she'll stop twisting the hell out of her hair.

"Oh." She exhales in an audible puff as she tilts her head back to look at me. She swallows. "I can't?"

"Nope."

"Then what are we doing? Why are you so nice to me? You're always so freaking nice to me, Boyd. And attentive. And good in bed. And—"

"We're just Chloe-and-Boyding." I cut her off before she gets any more worked up.

"Chloe-and-Boyding?"

"Yes," I say then brush my lips along the shell of her

ear. "Trust me, Chloe." I give her a gentle push back, because I'm not above distracting her with sex. Not one bit. I lie on the bed beside her and pull her to me. "And you can't go when there are so many fucks I haven't given you yet, Chloe. I'd like to give you all the fucks."

"All the fucks?" The tension eases from her body and her eyes flare, but in excitement instead of panic.

"All of them. The bossy fuck." I slip my hand under the hem of her shirt and lift it up and over her head. "The rough fuck." She lifts her hips as I grip the waistband of her leggings and tug. "The shower fuck." She sucks in a breath at that and swallows. "So many fucks, Chloe." I brush my lips against her ear. "The dirty talk fuck. The ass play fuck," I whisper. "Do you want to miss any of those?"

"No." She shakes her head and flexes her hips against me, already looking to move this forward. "I want all the fucks."

"Good. Then we're on the same page. Take off your bra."

I watch her slide a hand behind her back and unclasp it. It lands on the floor a second after my shirt.

"Don't move," I advise, holding up my hand before walking to my closet. When I come back she sits up on the bed, eyes wide.

"Is that your shoulder holster?"

I nod. I've never attempted to restrain a woman before with it, never wanted to, but I suspect Chloe will be game.

"Arms over your head," I tell her as I loop the holster in half and approach the bed. She nods eagerly, lying back and stretching her arms above her head. I don't have anything to attach this to, and I'm fairly certain she'll be able to wiggle out of this contraption if she wants to, but that's not the point.

She watches fascinated as I slip it over her wrists and tighten the adjustable straps.

"It's government-issued, right?" she asks, wetting her lips with her tongue.

This. Fucking. Girl.

"Absolutely," I agree and walk to the foot of the bed where I wrap my hands around her ankles and tug her towards me. She yelps, not expecting it. And I think she might meow when I prop her thighs on my shoulders. It's hard to quantify what that noise was. Could also have been coming from me. I really do enjoy having my face between her thighs.

I kiss the spot right above her mound then spread her lips apart with my thumbs and flick her clit with my tongue. But I'm just getting warmed up. Because I don't *like* doing this. I fucking love it.

I can physically see the reaction of her body from this position. Watch her get wet. And wetter. Listen to her soft sighs or the little humming noise she makes in the back of her throat, depending on what I'm doing. I can feel her calf muscles flex against my shoulders and watch as her knees draw closer to her in rhythm with her pussy clenching.

I get to watch every constriction of her opening as she reacts to my tongue and my lips and teeth when I lick and kiss and nip every inch of her. And I do. Adjusting to her every sigh and stretch. Reveling in every groan and arch of her back.

And she tastes fucking fantastic.

I will never get tired of doing this with her. Of seeing her with her walls down. Of watching her come and tasting the evidence of her excitement.

I slide my finger into her and watch her body close

around it, tight and hot. I stroke in and out a few times before sliding my wet fingertip to her ass and rimming her before gently applying pressure.

Her pussy clenches tightly at the first touch of my fingertip against her asshole, then immediately gets even wetter.

"You said you were curious, right?" I ask as my fingertip slides in.

"Yes," she hisses. Her back is arched and her hair is spread wantonly between her raised arms. Her legs have fallen off my shoulders and are splayed wide on the bed before me. "But maybe just your finger," she says on an exhale. "I really think you're too big. And I'm not just saying that to stroke your ego. It sorta feels like you barely fit in my, you know."

"In your pussy?" I ask between sucking on her clit and sliding my finger in deeper.

"Yeah, there." A soft hiss comes from her direction as she nods her head against the bedspread. "But I don't want to tell you how to do your job or anything."

"I appreciate the confidence," I reply with a laugh. "But I don't mind the feedback. I want to make sure I keep earning those five stars from you."

"Oh, you have been."

"Glad to hear it." God, her thighs are soft. I kiss her from her pussy to her knee before standing.

She's quiet for a second before two small words come out of her mouth.

"Have I?"

"Have you what?"

"Have I been earning five stars from you?" She says it softly, a hint of hesitation in her voice.

"Chloe, you don't even have to be in the room to earn five stars from me. Just the though of you when I'm jerking off in the shower earns you five stars."

"Like in Vail?" She tilts her head to the side and watches me as I cross over to the nightstand, biting her lip to try to block the smile on her face.

"Exactly like in Vail."

"So you were? You were jacking off in the shower thinking about me while I was in the next room?"

"Absolutely." I'm unabashed in my admittance.

"I didn't know," she murmurs. "And I still wasn't sure when you told me not to ask. I thought..." She trails off.

"You thought what?" I ask, as my pants hit the floor. I wrap a firm hand around myself without taking my eyes off of hers.

"I thought maybe you just liked long showers or maybe you were doing something in there, thinking about porn or someone who wasn't me."

"The first time I thought about you while touching myself was the morning after I met you in that detention room at the stadium."

"Really?" Her eyes flare and her bottom wiggles against the bed. "You did not!"

"Of course I did. I'm a guy."

She grins and buries her face in her arm, trying to hide her smile. "What do you think about when you do it?" She's looking at me again, a shy smile on her face. "What am I doing when you're thinking about me?"

"Anything. Everything. Sometimes you're on your knees sucking me off. Sometimes you're taking a shower while I watch." Her chest rises. She likes that. "Sometimes I'm pulling your hair"—her eyes widen at that—"and sometimes you're lying on my bed, asking me to come on your tits."

"Would you do that?" Her tongue darts out and wets her lips and she's pressed her legs together trying to get the friction she needs on her clit.

"Do what?"

"Come on me."

"Is that an invitation?"

"Yes." She nods. "I want you to. I want to watch."

Twenty-Three

Chloe

I really want to watch. I've never seen a guy get himself off before. Like actually jerk himself to release in front of me. I've given hand jobs, sure, but usually just long enough that the guy wanted to slap a condom on and get it inside of me.

Not to the point where I got to see him come. Actually see *it*.

The thought of Boyd doing this, touching himself while thinking of me, has me so hot and wet I think there might be a damp spot beneath me on his comforter. And I haven't even come yet.

So heck yes to watching. Plus, my hands are restrained so this is all on him. I feel no pressure whatsoever to make this good for him. This is nothing but pure hedonistic voyeurism for me.

He pours lube from a bottle in his nightstand onto his palm and grips himself without breaking eye contact. Then he straddles me on the bed, his knees bracketing my hips as he sits back on his ankles while tugging on his dick in one long slick pull. The head disappears as his hand reaches the top before popping back out as he slides it down to the base.

Beneath him, I cross my legs. It's almost involuntary

at first. But soon I'm squeezing my thighs tighter in some vain attempt to dry-hump myself while I watch him. This was a terrible idea. I wish my hands were free so I could touch myself while I watched, because this is torture. I can't touch him, I can't touch myself. Saliva pools on my tongue and I wish I could take him in my mouth right now. I swallow and lick my lips, thinking about what he'd taste like, how wide I'd have to stretch to accommodate him.

I close my eyes for just a moment and listen because the sound of his lubricated dick sliding though his hand and his shortened breaths are an erotic melody that I'd like to commit to memory forever. Except I can't take my eyes off of him. Off his dick. Off his strong hand. Off his eyes, watching me watch him. So I bit my lip and lock gazes with him.

Then he starts in with the dirty talk.

Telling me all the things he'd like to do with me. To me.

And now I'm positively writhing beneath him, my heels planted on the bed as I attempt to either buck him off of me or find a point of contact to rub myself against.

I'm begging him to finish. To come on me. And not because I want him to hurry so he can take care of me. But because it's so freaking hot watching him enjoy himself. His arm muscles flexing as he glides his hand up and down. His strokes so much faster than I'd be capable of doing for him. Rougher than I'd feel comfortable doing.

It turns me on seeing him turned on.

It feels powerful and I'm not even doing anything but observing as he kneels over me. Watching his hips flex when comes. Hearing him grunt his release. Feeling it hit my chest and seeing the look in his eyes when it does.

Because he's doing this looking at *me*. Thinking about *me*. How could I not be turned on by that?

"Fuck, Chloe." He pants above me, catching his breath. I moan low in my throat and raise my bound hands to him, my request silent. I need to touch him.

"Don't move," he instructs, dropping the holster on the floor beside the bed. A moment later he's back with a warm washcloth. Covering more skin than necessary. Long slow sweeps circling my breasts and tugging my nipples through the terrycloth. But I've had enough, I need to touch him. I sit up and pull his lips to mine.

"That was the hottest thing I've ever seen," I say between kissing him. I run my hands up and down his arms, my fingertips softly tracing his arms as I drop my lips to his neck, pressing kisses everywhere I can reach. Then I wind my fingers into his hair and tug, wondering if it feels as good to him as it does when he's done it to me.

"I love—" Oh, shit. "I like you, Boyd." I like him.

He's still for a moment before replying, his breath warm against my neck when he speaks.

"I *like* you too, Chloe."

Now I'm the one who's stilling. Did he just say *like* with an awful lot of meaning?

"Relax," he hums into my ear and I sigh into him as he rolls us over so he's on top. Then he coerces me into relaxation. With his mouth. He's not saying anything though. He's very effective with his lips without words.

"I have something for you," he says and I nod. I know he does, I can feel it against my thigh. "You distracted me before," he adds as he reaches into the nightstand and grabs the lube again.

Um. Okay, I guess we're really going there. I can try. I did tell him I was curious but I don't think it's gonna work. I exhale in relief when he pulls something else from the drawer.

"Are those, um…" I pause. I want him to say it. In case I'm wrong and he thinks I'm a total novice. Which I am, but better safe than sorry. Or what if it is what I think it is but he wants me to use it on him? I don't know if I can do that. But maybe he doesn't want to do that to me either? But he's the one who got it so I should probably stop arguing with myself and see what he says.

"Anal beads," he confirms and pops the cap of the lube. "You're still interested?" His brow is cocked in challenge but it's unnecessary. I'm interested.

They're small, and while they do increase in size as they go, the largest is still smaller than Boyd's finger. He's probably bought beginner beads. Fine. I've Googled it, okay? Just in case it ever came up, not because I'm a pervert or anything. Anyway, they're definitely beginner beads.

I nod my head silently and roll over when he motions for me to do so. I glance at him over my shoulder and then bury my face in the bedspread because I'm about to laugh out of nervousness. Are we really doing this?

Then he yanks my hips up until I'm on my knees, spread wide as he kneels between them, and I'm not thinking about laughing. And maybe I *am* a pervert because I'm throbbing in the best possible way. He rims my ass with his fingertip and I groan and roll my hips towards him, wanting more. But he just circles around and around while I writhe, ready to beg for it.

The first bead slips in and I feel it in my entire body. My chest tightens as I suck in a breath, then I relax and exhale and focus on how erotic it feels, having something in me in this way. He slides another bead in and I'm shocked to feel response in other places, somehow not expecting to be sexually excited in tandem. I'm not sure why I didn't, because every nerve ending in my body feels like an erogenous zone. My nipples are so hard they're throbbing and I think if he touched my clit right now I'd come. But it's not just the obvious places, I feel it everywhere. The back of my neck tingles and my stomach is tight. The curve of my lower back and the tips of my fingers. Everywhere.

I groan when he caresses the soft curve where my thigh meets my ass and bury my face in my hands when more lube drips onto my skin. He slips another bead in and the pressure is intense, a pleasurable intense. When his finger swirls my clit as the next bead slides in I moan and push back on my hands, arching my back and shoving my hips closer to him. When I finally hear the condom wrapper crinkle I want to weep with joy. With my vagina.

And then he's nudging at my entrance with his cock. I glance at him over my shoulder. He's got one foot on the floor and the other planted on the bed outside my knee, his eyes on the view in front of him. I imagine the end of the trail of beads hanging out of my ass and I clench so hard around his cock that he slaps my ass and tells me to, "Relax, Chloe."

It's sort of humiliating but it's working for me.

My fingers are clenching the bedspread as I feel him slide deeper. It's tighter this way, and he's a tight fit without any assistance. I feel oddly proud of the stretch. Of the heated words coming from Boyd. Of the fullness. My tits bounce as he pulls back and drives in, his hands on my hips, running down my spine, pulling my hair.

"You feel so good," I murmur, more to myself than to him. I'm clenching him so tightly I'm surprised he can still move. The sensation of having the beads in my ass while he's inside of me is not what I thought it'd be. It's better.

I'm sort of getting off on my bravery. On being adventurous—it's an ego boost.

And then he's sliding the beads out, and that's a whole different sensation. My pulse skyrockets and my head drops—as much as it can with Boyd still fisting a handful of my hair. My orgasm feels like it lasts forever and the insides of my thighs are soaked. Behind me Boyd's breaths have shallowed and then he jerks inside of me, two, three times before his pelvis comes to a rest flat against my ass. His skin is warm, the light trail of hair that runs from his belly button downward brushing against my bottom.

I feel a kiss press between my shoulder blades and then he pulls out of me and stands. The bed dips when he slides in behind me a minute later. I'm wrecked. Incredibly, gloriously wrecked. I love sex with Boyd. I don't think about anything else when he's touching me. My mind doesn't race with worries. I don't second-guess something he said an hour ago. I'm like, my best me when we're together.

"Stay," he murmurs into my ear, his lips brushing my jaw, his arm wrapping around my stomach.

So I stay. Relaxed, sated, happy.

But four hours later, I'm wide awake, unable to will myself back to sleep.

Boyd isn't touching me. He's rolled over, his arm flung across the bed, breathing deep and even. I turn on my side and watch the city over the half walls of the loft. Those floor-to-ceiling windows that Boyd promised offered a great view at night? They do. They also let the light in. You don't think about the light at two AM when you live on the eighth floor far above street lights. Boyd lives on the third and fourth floors. He has mechanical curtains, but I have no idea how to operate them. Maybe he always sleeps with them open? I don't think I could get used to that. Wait, I wonder if you can see in these windows? The building across the street isn't that far away. But I can't see anything happening over there, so I decide not to think about it.

Besides, there are so many other things to think about. What did he mean by stay? All night? Maybe he just didn't want to drive me home? Maybe he meant stay as in stay still, because he has a cuddling fetish. Maybe he was going to drive me home after, but he fell asleep.

I don't have a toothbrush. I don't have a toothbrush. I don't have a toothbrush. I. Do. Not. Have. A. Toothbrush. *Focus on that, Chloe.*

I flex my toes and turn back to look at the ceiling. I just need time to think. No, don't think. Just breathe.

Did he really want me to stay all night? The thing is, I'm awake now, so maybe I should just go. I should probably go. I spent all day with Boyd and I have lesson plans to work on, plus progress reports are coming up. And I was going to change my sheets. Also I'm having brunch with the girls tomorrow and I'll need to shower and change clothes.

Boyd has a shower and a dryer full of my clean clothes. But still, maybe I don't want to wear those clothes. And I don't have any makeup with me. I can't show up for brunch fresh from the shower with my hair in an air-dried ponytail. How do women spend the night so casually? Is everyone else carrying their makeup bag with them twenty-four seven, just in case? With a toothbrush? I don't keep my toothbrush in my makeup bag. Was there a memo about this stuff that I missed somewhere?

I should go.

I slip out of bed and find my clothes on the floor. I don't need the stuff in the dryer. I can get it... later. *The light from the windows is actually kinda helpful*, I think as I tiptoe down the stairs.

I leave a note on the kitchen island. *Early brunch with girls, took an Uber home*. Because I'm not a total nut case. I'm not going to walk home in the middle of the night. But I do wonder what in the hell I'm doing as I close the front door softly behind me.

Twenty-Four
Chloe

"Do you think she's okay without me?" Sophie taps her fingertips against the cloth-covered table while perched on the end of her seat as if she's ready to jump up at a moment's notice. "She's asleep, and Luke is probably more qualified to take care of her than I am," she continues. "But I'm her mom. What if she needs me and I'm not there?"

"She's upstairs, Sophie. You are literally still in the same building," Everly points out. The four of us—Sophie, Everly, Sandra and myself—are having brunch at the new restaurant in Sophie's building. It's changed ownership since the last time we ate here because life is full of changes. Huge, terrifying changes that you can't seem to control. Changes that might alter the rest of your life.

Or possibly people just didn't like the menu. I don't know. On the plus side, the new place serves brunch.

"It's a really big building, Everly. What if the power goes out and I have to run up thirty-two flights to get to her?"

"Well, Luke would still be with her while you were running up the stairs, so I think it would be okay," Sandra reassures her. Today's the first time Sophie's left the baby since she was born.

"She's only forty-two days old. Do you think I'm a bad mom for leaving her to have lunch?" Sophie darts glances at the three of us before eyeing the door. "Oh, my God, my phone!" Her eyes widen as she digs her phone out of her purse and then she visibly relaxes as she holds up the screen. "Everly, why are you calling me?"

"To explain how a phone works. Now put it down next to your fork. If Luke needs you, he'll call."

"I'm ridiculous, aren't I?" Her chair scrapes against the floor as she finally scoots it all the way in to the table and relaxes. She shakes her head and exhales. "Okay, I'm fine. I've got this." She glances at her phone and laughs. "She probably won't even wake up for another hour."

We all take a collective sigh of relief and open our menus so that when the waitress asks us for the third time if we're ready to order, we will be.

"So, how are the POD's?" Everly directs the conversation to me after we've ordered and everyone's been served coffee.

"Um, you know, I haven't really gotten any lately." That's not entirely true. I probably have a bunch, I just haven't bothered to open my dating app in weeks.

"What'd you do? Close your accounts?"

Sort of.

"No, just busy. You know how it is."

"So men just stopped sending dick pics to you?" Everly asks, her tone dubious as if I'm lying.

"POD's! Everly, keep it classy." I need her to stop focusing on me. "I think the POD thing caught on and they all realized how stupid it was to text their junk to random women." I shrug.

"Really?" Her tone is dry. A quick glance at Sandra and Sophie tells me they're not buying what I'm selling either.

"Yup. I bet there's a group text. Between all the single guys in Philly. Agreeing that dick pics are stupid and banding together to stop sending them." I do a little fist-pump into the air to accentuate this win for women.

And then my phone rings.

My phone which I pulled out when Sandra asked me what level I was on in Pokemon and then left lying on the table between me and Everly.

My phone which has Boyd's phone number programmed into it.

My phone which is currently ringing, with an incoming call from Boyd lighting up the screen.

Why couldn't his name have been Sam? I could have played off a Sam or an Alex as anyone.

I make a grab for the phone but I'm too late. Way too late.

Because I've also assigned the picture that Boyd and I took together on top of Vail Mountain to his contact in my phone. So that's what's showing on the screen, behind the text spelling out his name and phone number for anyone close enough to read it. Everly's close enough to read it.

I hit the ignore call button but not before I catch the look of surprise on her face. At least there's that. I don't think I've ever managed to surprise her before. I enjoy that victory for the half a second she allows before she regains her composure and grins like that cat that ate the canary. Or the girl who's just figured out that you might be up to something with that guy she spent close to a year trying to hook you up with while you refused. It's pretty much the same grin.

"You're dating Sophie's brother."

"No way!" Sophie bursts out. "No freaking way."

"We're not dating!" I object, turning the ringer off and stuffing the phone in my bag before it can betray me any further.

"So you just happen to have his number programmed into your phone?" Everly deadpans. "With a picture of the two of you?"

"A picture!" Sophie gasps and slaps a hand over her mouth in surprise.

"Yup, with mountains in the background," Everly informs Sophie. "Which is weird. We don't have any mountains in Philadelphia…" She trails off, waiting for me to fill in the blanks.

"Not dating." I shake my head and tug on my left ear. My heart is starting to race.

"So why is he calling you?" Everly asks. But it's Everly, so it's really a demand for information posed as a question.

"Wait, how long has this been going on?" Sophie interjects. "Because I tried to set him up with you two weeks ago and he blew me off."

"Um, thanks?" I say and fiddle with a sweetener packet while they all stare at me. I consider telling them that we met at the hospital the day Christine was born like they assume, but I end up confessing the entire story about meeting Boyd the day prior when my date was arrested at the stadium.

"So Boyd blackmailed you into being his date to a wedding," Everly summarizes.

"Sort of, yeah. It was more of a favor."

"Because someone like Boyd would have a hard time finding a date," she adds, pinning me with a look that asks if I'm really this obtuse.

That point has always bothered me, but I tell them what he told me. "He didn't want to bring a real date because she'd read into it. Think he was introducing her to his family and stuff. Expect things."

"So he brought you instead. And introduced you to his family and stuff."

"Yes," I admit.

"At an out-of-town wedding."

"Yeah." I know what's coming next.

"Did you sleep with him?"

Called that.

"Um, well…" I shred the sweetener packet before remembering that it's full and end up with a pile of sugar on my hands. "Yes," I admit. "But that part wasn't a favor," I add in a rush. Just in case there's any confusion.

"Was it good sex?" Everly asks, leaning forward and tucking her hair behind her ear.

I nod, my face down, concentrating on pushing the sugar into a pile. Which is nearly impossible on a cloth table cover, by the way.

"And then what?" she presses. "The wedding was a month ago and he's still calling you."

"We hang out and stuff." I shrug my shoulder and stab some eggs with my fork.

"Yeah, that's called dating," Everly deadpans.

"No, it's not like that." I take a bite but no one changes the subject while I chew. Clearly I'm not getting out of talking about this. Has it really been a month since the wedding? "It was like, I owed him a favor and then he owed me a favor."

Sandra's eyes widen and Everly murmurs, "Uh huh." Sophie gives me an 'are you serious' raised eyebrow.

"Sometimes we grab something to eat together."

"Also called a date." Everly nods her head while I reply, "No," and shake mine.

"Once he helped me drag home a bookcase I found at

a garage sale. And we went to a flea market together. That kind of stuff."

"That's called a boyfriend," Everly says, not blinking.

"No." I shake my head again. "We're just Chloe-and-Boyding." Holy shit, that makes no sense. Why did it make sense when Boyd said it?

"Is he seeing anyone else?" This is from Sandra.

"No," I whisper. "I don't think so." We haven't talked about it, but I know he's not. Besides, he's always with me. I don't know when he'd have the time to be with someone else. Oh, my God. Have I been dating Boyd this entire time? Without knowing it?

"And you closed your online dating profiles, didn't you?"

"No!" I object. "I didn't. I just haven't opened them since we went to New York," I add in a muffled sigh. Not muffled enough because Everly is all over that.

"You went to New York together too?"

"Just that one time, for the day. To find a dress for the wedding."

"Yeah. All that is called dating." She waves a finger in the air. "You're dating Boyd."

I think I'm going to throw up.

"You might even be engaged," Everly continues. "For all you know."

Is that what I want? To be dating Boyd? What if it doesn't end well? Sophie's his sister—and one of my best friends. It would be awkward if it didn't end well. It's already awkward. And I don't want it to end.

"Why didn't you ask him to do the career day thing at your school next month?" Sophie questions.

"What?" I stare at her blankly.

"He seemed kinda put out that you didn't ask him to do it. It didn't make any sense to me at the time," she

212

says. "Since I didn't know you were secretly dating," she adds, drily.

"He's probably worried that he's your sidepiece," Everly pipes in. "Since you don't invite him to anything," she adds, examining her manicure. "Hey, are you pregnant by any chance? Remember how Sophie didn't know she was pregnant? That might be a thing you can add to your collection of things you don't know are happening." Her eyes light up and she places a hand on her chest. "Can I be the godmother?"

"I'm not pregnant." But I do feel sick.

Twenty-Five
Chloe

I'm so confused. Has Boyd been lying to me all this time? Does he think we're dating? And since when? Has he always thought we were dating? Why lie about it? All this favor stuff and being nice and making me fall in love with him on the sly. Maybe I have been living in a bubble of denial, but Boyd's been lying. Right? *I need a favor, Chloe. I like you, Chloe. Pretend with me, Chloe.* What parts were real?

I look up, startled to see that I'm at Boyd's. I don't remember walking here. I remember leaving lunch, but did I really just walk a mile without seeing anything? I hover on the sidewalk, unsure of what I'm doing. I stare at my feet on the pavement and bounce my toes inside of my shoes before pulling open the door. I make it into the lobby before remembering that I've never been here without Boyd, and this is a secure building, meaning I can't make it past the lobby without a key or getting buzzed in or whatever. And I don't even know if he's home right now.

"Miss Scott, did you need to be buzzed through?"

I turn to look at the concierge, a tall distinguished-looking man in his fifties. I've seen him before, a bunch of times, but I don't think I've ever spoken to him. Actually, I know I haven't because I think I just detected an English accent, and I'd've remembered that. How the heck does he know my name?

"I'm here to see a resident," I stammer, unsure of how to proceed.

"Of course, Miss Scott. You're on Mr. Gallagher's list. I'll buzz you through."

I'm on his list. Another thing I didn't freaking know about.

I skip the elevator in favor of the stairs. He's only two flights up and honestly? I have no idea what I'm going to say to him when I get there.

But I don't have long to think about it because he's waiting for me at the door. Apparently the buzzing through service includes a heads up to the tenant.

He's leaning against the frame, watching me walk down the hall towards him. His arms are crossed against his chest. He's in another one of the shirts he got that day we went to New York and a pair of faded well-worn jeans. When I get closer I also see he's annoyed, his eyes dull and his expression guarded.

Wait.

Is he mad at *me*? Oh, heck, no.

Because I'm mad at *him*.

And really, is there anything more annoying than someone who's mad at you when you're the one who's supposed to be mad? No. No, there is not.

"Nice of you to come back," he comments. The muscle in his jaw flexes and then he pushes off the doorframe and rubs his jaw with his hand, following me into his loft.

"What is with all the lies, Boyd?" I've managed to make it through lunch with the girls without having a complete freakout. No, I've saved that for Boyd. So I ignore his annoyance and dive in with my own.

"What?" Surprise crosses his face. His forehead creases and his face softens. "Chloe, what are you talking about?"

"Us!" I cry. "The favors were all a lie, right? You didn't need a date for that wedding, did you? You probably cancelled on some other girl to take me." His brow lifts a fraction when I say that and I know I'm right. "Offering to help me with my dating skills? Bringing me donuts and giving me all those life-altering orgasms?" He smiles at this and it just pisses me off. "Do not smile at me, Boyd. Don't! I don't know what is real and what is a lie with you. Are we dating? What the hell does Chloe-and-Boyding even mean? Does it mean friends with benefits? Does it mean you're my boyfriend?"

"I think you know there's something here, Chloe." He says it softly, like he's trying to calm me down. "Between us."

"Well, I think you need to think about that," I snap back. "Maybe I'm not capable of what you want from me."

"I think you are." He looks directly at me, his gaze unwavering. "I know you are."

"I don't know what I'm supposed to think," I say, waving my hands because I'm starting to get panicky. No. I was past panicky an hour ago. I'm headed straight towards somewhere I don't want to go and something I don't want him to see.

"It's pretty simple, Chloe." His tone is gentle. "Don't believe the lies. Trust me. Trust the way I make you feel. Trust me when I tell you that I love you."

Oh, God.

I feel like the rest of my life is teetering on this moment. And it's too much. I need a freaking second, but Boyd is standing here looking for answers.

His cell phone rings—the ringtone one I recognize. It's the one assigned to work—the one he always has to take. He groans and answers it, muttering a terse, "One second," into the phone before holding it at his side and pulling me onto one of the stools at his kitchen island. A glass of water is set in front of me and he tells me to breathe and give him one second before turning his back and barking into the phone.

Obviously that's when I get the hell out.

I'm shaking. My heart is racing so fast and my breathing is heavy. I'm having a panic attack. I swallow hard and my eyes burn. My throat is tight as I fight back the threatening tears because for me, a bad panic attack makes me sob too. As if the rest of it wasn't bad enough, the threat of tears is always the final insulting straw. I hate the feeling before crying. Actual tears aren't as bad as that moment before, when the throbbing starts behind my eyes and I feel ashamed for crying on top of everything else.

I know it's likely Boyd will follow me, and I don't want him to see me like this. I don't want anyone to see me like this. Not ever. It's been years since I had a panic attack. Since I moved into the dorms freshman year. I got there a few hours before Everly and after my mom left I lost it. Everly wasn't there yet, I was alone in a new place about to start a new chapter and I don't know, I just lost it. And it's stupid, right? I was about to start college with my best friend by my side. A great college that I wanted to go to, was thrilled to be at and was qualified to excel in academically. I had nothing to be unhappy about. Yet I sat in that dorm room feeling like all the air got sucked out of the room and the walls were closing in on me.

I felt alone even though the halls were bustling with people just outside my door. But what good does that do?

When you're surrounded by people who wouldn't understand? Who don't really know you? Maybe they'd want to help or maybe they'd think you were a drama llama. A hot mess they'd want to steer away from for the rest of the year.

So I focused on the empty bulletin board over my desk and breathed. In and out, in and out until it subsided. And then I calmly unpacked all my things and put my bed together. Fixed my makeup and quietly left the dorm to take a walk, my chest still tight, my shoulders heavy. I ended up in the campus library, where I walked up and down the aisles of books and fought off all the fears that were threatening to strangle me and focused on how lucky I was to be there.

So I do now what I did then. I hide.

I know what route he'd expect me to take and I take the opposite. I exit the building through a side door that bypasses the lobby that you can't enter from the outside. I make it the two blocks to the Starbucks I saw him in all those weeks ago and lock myself in the bathroom.

I lean against the door and wrap my arms around myself, focusing on the hand dryer on the opposite wall. *You're not gonna die, Chloe. Just breathe. It'll pass in a few minutes.*

I hope.

Twenty-Six
Chloe

"I feel like an idiot."

I'm at Everly's condo, tucked on her sofa under a blanket while she talks me off the proverbial ledge. I came straight here after I managed to calm down enough to leave the Starbucks bathroom.

"You're the least idiotic person I know," Everly says, her face earnest.

I'm in love with Boyd.

It's sort of terrifying.

It's sort of exhilarating.

"Was it as scary for you as it is for me? Falling for Sawyer?"

"Not really, no." She shakes her head. "I'm sure I had some of the same worries, everyone does. But I'm a leaper. You're a thinker. We process things differently."

"You didn't have a panic attack and run away?" I ask sarcastically.

"No," she muses. "Not even that time he refused to have sex with me."

"That was your first date, Everly. And you did have sex," I remind her. I know, because I heard about it for a week.

"Whew." She blows out a breath. "It was a tough few

hours though. How is Boyd's POD by the way? Can we talk about that?" She leans forward on the couch, looking at me expectantly.

"Um, no. I don't think so."

She shrugs good-naturedly then changes the subject back to me. "Chloe, why didn't you tell me you were struggling with your anxiety? You know I'm never too busy for you, no matter how many husbands or children I have."

"You have one husband, babe," Sawyer says, walking into the room at that moment.

"You're still the one, baby."

"We've been married for three months, Everly. I sure as hell better still be the one."

"Sawyer," she sighs. "I was trying to have a moment, okay? Work with me."

"Next time, try waiting more than a day after downloading Shania Twain's greatest hits to your iPod. You do realize the receipts come to my email, don't you?"

"Um." Everly looks away and scrunches her nose. "No?"

"You've been on quite the 90's love ballads kick this week. Which is weird, because you're not old enough to have owned the CD's those songs were originally released on." He looks at her with amused interest.

"What's a CD?" She blinks at Sawyer dramatically.

"Cute. Keep it up."

"Nineties music is all the rage with the millennials," she tells him with a shrug. "I saw a blog post about it."

"Don't worry, sweets. We'll beat the odds together." He winks and she scowls. "You're still the only one I dream of," he calls as he walks into the kitchen and grabs a bottle of water.

"See! I don't even care that you lifted that from a song. It still gave me all the feels!"

I tune out Everly and Sawyer and think back to the day that Boyd walked into Starbucks and crashed my date. What would I have done if he'd simply asked me to go to that wedding with him? If he hadn't told me that it was a favor?

I'd have gone. I would have, I think. Maybe? I'd have wanted to. Absolutely I'd have wanted to. But I'd have been intimidated and anxious. A basket case. A nervous wreck of joke-telling from beginning to end. I would not have been myself. I mean, the basket-case joke-telling is me, but it's not my best me.

Or would I have said no? Deflected his interest just to avoid the anxiety of a date with Boyd? I'd absolutely have said no if I'd known it was a two-night trip. If I'd had time to think about that? Ahead of time? No way. I'd have worried about it for two weeks. I'd have imagined ten different ways I could have embarrassed myself. Gotten myself worked up about situations that might or might not even take place. The anxiety would have suffocated me.

And he knew that. He saw my awkward joke-telling disaster of a date for what it was—social anxiety. And he figured out a way for us to get to know each other in a way that would work for me. He catered this entire courtship around me. And if that isn't love, I don't know what is.

And it hits me like a ton of bricks. Which is a stupid analogy because if a ton of bricks hit you, it'd hurt. Hmm, maybe the analogy does work, because the idea of spending another second without telling Boyd that I love him does hurt. Whatever could go wrong with us, it's better than being without him. All the fears, all of them—

I'll figure them out. Boyd is the one. *My one.* And none of the rest of it matters.

"Wait, what's happening?" Everly questions as I jam my arms into my jacket. "Where are you going?"

"Boyd's. I love him, I'm an idiot and I have to talk to him." My hand trembles as I stuff my phone in my pocket, but I'm not giving in to the fear. I'm trusting the love.

"Chloe, wait. You need a plan!" Everly jumps off the couch and follows me to the door. "Like... take him to Vegas and elope!" She claps her hands in delight and her eyes sparkle.

I laugh as my purse swings over my shoulder. "Thanks, but that seems a little dramatic. I'm going to keep it simple—tell him that I love him."

"That's a good plan too, Chloe." Her face softens and she wraps her arms around me. "You got this, bestie."

She slaps me on the ass as I leave with a, "Go get 'em, tiger!" I shake my head and laugh, waving as the door closes.

Twenty-Seven
Chloe

When I hit the sidewalk outside of Everly's I nearly run smack into Boyd leaning against his car, parked at the curb.

"Boyd, I was just…" I pause, wondering what he's thinking and where I should start. "I was just heading back to your place."

"No need. I came to get you," he replies. His posture is relaxed, hands in his pockets, but his eyes look strained. "You didn't answer your phone."

"I'm sorry, I turned it off at brunch this morning, it's been in my purse all day on silent." I am really messing up today. "How did you know I was here?"

"I tried Sophie first, who incidentally would like to set us up." The corner of his lip curves. "Then she called Everly and found out you were on your way down so I swung over here instead."

"Wow. You must really like me." I can't keep the smile from pulling at my cheek.

"Why's that?"

"Now you're gonna have to live with Everly having your phone number."

"I figured I'd have to change it."

I laugh then draw in a breath. Here goes.

"I need a favor."

"What's that?"

"I need to tell you a joke."

"Okay." He inclines his head with a half smile but the worry has left his eyes.

"Knock, knock."

"Who's there?"

"I love."

"I love who?"

"I love you too." Then I start giggling. "That was so bad!" I exclaim. "Like the worst!" I'm laughing so hard I'm crying. "How have you put up with me for this long?"

"Because I love you," he says and I sink into him as he wraps his arms around me. "It was pretty bad though." His grip on me loosens. "Hold on while I text that to myself so I can remember it forever."

"Stop. That was practice. Let me do it again."

"Okay." The smile reaches his eyes now.

"Boyd Gallagher, I love you."

We both eye each other for a moment and then he smiles. "I don't know, I might want to keep the first one. The first one was so perfectly you."

"You can have both of them."

"Deal."

Epilogue

Chloe

Being a teacher has some perks. Two weeks off at Christmas is one of them. Two weeks about to be put to very good use spending the holiday in Vail with my boyfriend. Yeah, I still do a little 'raise the roof' happy dance when I think about Boyd being my boyfriend. But only in my head. I stopped doing it in front of people. Most of the time.

I felt a moment of guilt about not going home for Christmas, but I got over it. Boyd met my mom at Thanksgiving and we had dinner with my dad the following weekend, so I feel like I checked off any responsibility I had there. I think it's okay for me to be little selfish and spend the holiday in a snowy cocoon with my boyfriend. How many opportunities will we have to spend two whole weeks together sipping hot cocoa and snuggling by the fire? Just the two of us?

"Babe, why are you doing that weird dance?"

"No reason," I reply, dropping my arms.

"Really?" Boyd smirks. "What were you thinking about?"

"If you must know, it's my candy plane dance." It's not. It's my boyfriend dance. A teeny-tiny lie never hurt anybody.

227

"Your candy plane dance?"

"Yup." I'm holding firm on this. "I really, really love the candy plane," I say, dropping into his lap. We're currently on the plane somewhere over Nebraska. We should be in Vail within a couple of hours.

"Do you?"

"I do. It's so sexy and well equipped," I purr into his ear. "And big. Much bigger than I expected." I slide my hand behind his neck and rub the skin there. I love touching him. "And let's face it. No one wants to be stuck flying in the middle seat on Southwest," I finish with a giggle.

"I knew exactly where that was going," he says, slipping his fingers under the back of my shirt and trailing them lightly along my spine.

"You always do," I agree, touching my forehead to his. He's always touching me too and I love it. I'm officially team touchy-feely. Team public displays of affection. Team mile-high club. Team Boyd. I'm not team winter sports though, which reminds me… "You know I don't know how to ski, right?"

"I'll teach you." His eyes light up when he smiles like this, shining with unspoken promises.

"You do have a bit of a teacher fetish, don't you?" I smile back, pressing myself into his chest. "You love teaching me new things. Naughty things." I rub myself against him and wonder exactly how far over Nebraska we are. I'm not sure I can wait.

"Only with you." He nips my earlobe between his teeth, which is always a straight shot to my clit.

"Do you think the pilots need to use the restroom or get a snack or something?"

"Who knows," he replies, apparently unconcerned. Is he really not getting this?

"Boyd," I sigh and, placing a hand on his chest, push myself back a few inches and widen my eyes suggestively.

"Safety girl, are you suggesting we have sex on the candy plane? Do you really think it's safe to unbuckle our seat belts while in flight?"

"Um…" Oh. Boyd's relaxed in his seat as if he has no intention of taking me up on my illicit in-flight offer, his legs sprawled beneath me, his neck resting against the headrest behind him. "Well, I'm willing to risk it." I shrug. "Take off your pants."

A couple of hours later we land at the regional airport. We stop again at the Red Canyon Cafe for breakfast on our way to Vail. Snow is falling this time, making the trip slower, but we're not in any hurry. We get a window table at the cafe and after ordering sit back to watch the snowfall. It's magical. All of it—the snow, the location, being in love, life.

I found a great therapist and I'm learning how to better manage my anxiety before it gets the best of me. Because life is full of stress, even good stress. Engagements, weddings, babies, new homes. All of those events are thrilling, yet not stress-free. And I know they're all in my future with Boyd. And I know I'm never going to adapt to change the way some people do, and that's okay, because Boyd gets me and he knows I need a minute (or an hour) to adjust. And he loves me enough to give that to me without judgement.

I've had to work through feeling guilty over my anxiety, feeling guilty for being anxious about things I'm excited about. Some of the best things in life are stressful. Being anxious about them doesn't mean I'm not grateful to be experiencing them—it's just part of who I am and how I process. Knowing that Boyd isn't judging me helps with the anxiety. A lot. Knowing unequivocally that he's on my side is everything.

"What do snowmen have for breakfast?" I hide my smile behind the rim of my coffee mug.

"Wait, are you nervous about something or are we doing a re-enactment of our first trip here?"

I lower my mug and laugh. "Re-enactment."

"Okay, what do snowmen have for breakfast?"

"Frosted flakes!" I laugh. "I just learned that one yesterday from my class."

"Nice," he agrees. "What falls in the winter but never gets hurt?"

"Boyd Gallagher, are *you* telling *me* a joke?"

"Yup." He grins.

He really loves me.

"A penguin?"

He shakes his head.

"A polar bear?"

"Snow. Snow falls in the winter and never gets hurt."

"Good one."

"Thanks." He gives me the lazy grin that does all the things to me and I can't wait to get him back to the hotel. And when I eat breakfast a little faster than usual he just tilts his head and looks on in amusement.

We pull up to the valet at the Arrabelle a short time later and I'm excited to see that we're staying at the same hotel as last time. Another fun memory to repeat.

Only this time we bypass check-in and head straight for the elevators. Weird. But I didn't see him check in last time either. He dropped me at the spa and checked us in after. I think.

"Do they have advance check-in here?" I ask as the elevator rises. "How did you get the key?" The elevator stops and Boyd holds the door while I exit and then leads us to the left.

"I actually own a unit here," he says casually as he inserts a key into a lock and turns it.

Wait.

"What do you mean you own a unit?"

"The Arrabelle is half condo, half hotel," he says as if this might keep me from asking more questions. It won't. The door swings open and my suspicions are confirmed. The condo is huge. The view stunning, blah blah. What I'm really interested in right now are the bedrooms. As in plural.

"If you own this, why didn't we stay here last time? Why did you pay for a hotel room in the same building you own a condo in?"

"Chloe," he says, shutting the door behind us. "I think that's obvious."

"Say it."

"This place has too many bedrooms." He can't even pretend not to smile.

"You lying liar who lies!" I point my finger at him. "You said that room we stayed in was all they had left!"

"Did I?"

"The room with the one bed!"

"Humph." He nods. "Technically it might have been the only room they had left for rental. I'm not sure since all I inquired about was reserving a room with one bed."

I gasp dramatically while trying to fight off the giggles that want to break out.

"I don't know that I ever said, 'Chloe, I do *not* own a condo sitting empty on the fifth floor,'" he offers.

"Well, that's true." I shrug. "You've got me there."

"Good, then we can move onto something that *you've* been omitting."

"What have I been omitting?" I ask, genuinely

confused.

"Your handcuff fetish," he says solemnly.

"My handcuff fetish?" I question, but yes, please.

He nods. "I think we both know how eager you were for me to slap some cuffs on you that day we met." He's closed the distance between us and is running his fingers lightly over my arm down to my wrist. It makes me tingle with excitement, everywhere.

"Please tell me this conversation ends with you telling me that you packed handcuffs." My pulse is racing a little bit just thinking about it. I hope he's not teasing me, because we're here for two weeks and I don't think they sell handcuffs down at the ski shop. "Real ones," I add.

"Chloe, of course they're real. Trust me."

Oh, I do.

The Complete Series

WRONG: Sophie & Luke
RIGHT: Everly & Sawyer
FLING: Sandra & Gabe
TRUST: Chloe & Boyd

Acknowledgements

Well, it's over. Just over a year ago I published Wrong, with no long term game plan. I just felt compelled to write that story about a girl and her gynecologist, and so I did. I'd never written anything before, and I wasn't sure I would ever write anything again, but then people *liked* Wrong. I could go on for pages about how that *feels*, but you're probably sick of hearing it. (It feels like a bouquet of joy, gratitude, unicorns and an orange kitten.)

But Trust is the end of the "Wrong" series. I've never classified them as a series - I consider them all standalones about four different couples that cross over into each other's lives. The timelines of Wrong, Right & Fling are all happening at the same time. The only one I'm iffy on is Trust, because the previous characters are all living their happily ever afters during the timeline of Trust, but there is no continuing storyline throughout the books.

Chloe. Gah, I was nervous about her. I *am* nervous about her since I have to type these notes up *before* Trust publishes. Will you accept her? Will you "get" her? Was Boyd too perfect? Will you hate me for making you wait until 50 or 60% for the sex?!?! (It's hard to tell at this moment where it will fall percentage wise on your device, but I know it's late!) I struggled with that. I had more than one conversation with my bestie Kristi about that...

"Kristi, the sex is taking forever in this book. I don't think I can make the sexing happen until like... half way through." I say, nervously listening to the dead silence on the other end of the line.

"Are you freaking serious?"

"I know!"

"You're the one that gets pissed off when authors make *you* wait past the 30% mark!"

"I know!" I agree, sadly. It's actually the 25% mark, but that correction is not in my favor, so I keep that to myself. "It's just... don't make me say it."

"What?"

"It just didn't make sense to the story! Okay?! Chloe's just... she's... there's just no reasonable way that this girl is having sex with Boyd any earlier."

"Huh," Kristi mutters. "Okay, well it's *your* rule that you're breaking."

"I know. I want to punch myself in the face too."

So I apologize for the delayed sexual gratification in Trust. And I hope you were able to understand Chloe, even if you don't relate to having anxiety issues.

What's next? I have one idea that's been percolating in my head for the last year and one idea that just popped into my head in the last two weeks. And that's all I can say about that for now. ☺

I am so grateful for your support and encouragement. It blows me away each time someone gives me a few hours of their time to read my words. THANK YOU. Every time you spread the word about a release: share a post, like a post, leave a review, or tell a friend you enjoyed reading one of my books, it's a big deal. A huge deal. I cannot do this without *you*.

Kristi, thank you for being my BAE!
Franziska, thank you for caring enough to constantly ask if TRUST was done. ☺
Chelcie, thank you for the amazeball stories…

Shameless plea for you to join my newsletter where you'll always be notified of new releases, special offers, signing events & any other fun things I can come up with!

I've started a reader group on Facebook! It's called the Grind Me Cafe in honor of the place where the series started. I post teasers and giveaways in there so if you're interested, join us! Facebook Group: bit.ly/2eXkdpA

Thank you,
Jana

Follow me on Social Media

Facebook: Jana Aston
Twitter: @janaaston
Website: Janaaston.com
Instagram: SteveCatnip

About Jana

Jana Aston is the New York Times bestselling author of WRONG.

She's normally a very cautious and practical person, but after writing Wrong she said fuck it and quit her super boring day job to write more books. She's hoping that was not a stupid idea. In her defense, it was a really boring job.

Made in the USA
Columbia, SC
17 September 2017